IN LIEU OF FLOWERS

KEITH STEINBAUM

This is a work of fiction. Names, characters, places, and incidents are products of the author's imagination or are used fictitiously and are not to be construed as real. Any resemblance to actual events, locations, organizations, or persons, living or dead, is entirely coincidental.

World Castle Publishing, LLC
Pensacola, Florida
Copyright © 2024 Keith Steinbaum
Hardback ISBN: 9798891261648
Paperback ISBN: 9798891261655
eBook ISBN: 9798891261662
First Edition World Castle Publishing, LLC, March 26, 2024
http://www.worldcastlepublishing.com

Cover: Cover Designs by Karen
https://www.cover-designs-by-karen.com
Editor: Randy at Kirkus

Inspired by the life and murder of my grandfather, Charles
Jacobson:
- A stolen baby in Romania
- An American WWI veteran
- A fatal victim of a robbery in Boyle Heights, California —
city of
Evergreen Cemetery

Contents

PROLOGUE

From Wikipedia:
Strigoi in Romanian mythology are troubled spirits that are said to have risen from the grave. They are attributed with the abilities to transform into an animal, become invisible, and to gain vitality from the blood of their victims. It is related to the Romanian verb a striga, which means "to scream."

***

In 1926, at the peak of Prohibition, enough reports about what a Los Angeles Times article described as "unearthly shrieks, laughter, and weird scurrying" coming from Evergreen Cemetery caused Police Captain Bond of the LAPD to become suspicious of activity other than the rumors of ghosts — a topic of concern among the locals. Bond and other men waited until nightfall before silently making their way past many graves until finally reaching the cottage of the superintendent in the center of the cemetery. To their amazement, they entered a well-organized speakeasy containing barrels of whiskey and wine, replete with glasses arranged in orderly rows.

After shutting down the illegal operation, including the additional discovery of fifty gallons of wine hidden in a hearse in an adjacent barn, Captain Bond remarked, "There are no more spirits in Evergreen Cemetery. Though there may be a few ghosts for all I know."

Not yet, Captain Bond. But they're coming.

CHAPTER ONE
THE THEFT

Bucharest, Romania, 1920

The descending late autumn sun, fighting a losing battle against the advancing hordes of encroaching clouds, offered an opportune moment for the theft of the baby to succeed. Gunari's watchful, brown Roma eyes peered out from the safeguarding shadows of an empty doorway in preparation for the deed. Inhaling and exhaling in a slow and rhythmic attempt at calming his nerves, he gazed northward toward the glorious yet fading outline of the Bucegi mountains, seeking the strength he needed to pounce, steal, and escape.

A mere three days before, no such thought of attempting anything of this magnitude existed in Gunari's mind. Riding into town on his wagon that day, he mumbled to himself in frustration over his tardiness caused by an old horse in the stages of going lame. Promising his client the delivery of mended shoes before his late arrival time, he received a tongue-lashing and an unveiled threat to seek another cobbler. Fearing the loss of business, something Gunari couldn't afford with a baby on the way, he lessened the agreed-upon price of the repair, settling for half the original amount.

Seething and cursing his fate as he returned to his wagon, a dour-faced yet well-dressed stranger approached him in the street.

"Could I interest you in making some money?" the man asked.

Turning around to respond, Gunari felt an immediate sense of discomfort looking into the man's dark, cavernous eyes, staring at him with an intensity that seemed both questioning and condemning. Without understanding why, and despite his sudden unease, Gunari experienced a strange inability to turn away from the stranger's penetrating gaze, which gave the impression of looking through him rather than at him. Wearing a black, cone-shaped sheepskin hat, an embroidered, knee-length white linen shirt, pleated black trousers, and black-and-red leather shoes, the man appeared to have money. Curious and vulnerable, Gunari asked, "What do you have in mind?"

The man smiled and took a step closer before pointing toward the horse.

"I couldn't help noticing his crooked stance," he said. "Your horse is wearing down, and those legs are getting weak. Anyone who knows horses could tell you that the poor thing doesn't have much left to give."

"You're telling me something I already know, mister," Gunari said. "But it costs a lot of money for a horse, the kind of money I don't have. You plan on offering me that much?"

The man tilted his head and winked.

"How about enough to buy a strong, young Gypsy

Vanner?" he asked. "And not only that, still have money left over to buy a whole new set of cobbler's tools, which I'm sure you need as well."

Gunari's mouth dropped a slight bit, taken aback by the unexpected offer to make enough money to purchase the most desirable horse around. Listening to the stranger's dialect, one containing an accent spoken near the border of Bulgaria, where Gunari's Vlach Romani community previously lived, offered a possible clue as to his background.

"How did you know I need new tools?" he asked.

"I know things, Gunari," the man replied, speaking in a calm yet assertive tone.

Gunari's eyes narrowed. "How did you know my name?"

"I know many names of the Vlach Romani," he answered. "But what's important is my offer and whether you'll take me up on it."

"Go ahead," Gunari said. "I'm listening."

"I want you to kidnap a baby," the man told him. "A specific male baby that I've chosen."

Gunari gasped, his eyes widening in startled disbelief.

"What?" he cried. "Steal a baby? I couldn't do that."

"Even knowing how much your life will change for the better?" the man asked. "Do you think another opportunity like this will ever come along? A new horse, new tools, and a future of great promise for your growing family."

"Why do you say my growing family?" Gunari asked. "Have you been spying on me?"

"Just listen to what I tell you," the man replied. "You will deliver the baby to me in the Băneasa Forest near your campground. Follow the winding path for about twenty minutes, and you'll come to a small field of grass before the trees continue. I'll be waiting there with the money."

The man smiled as he peered into Gunari's eyes. "Waiting with the money and with expectations."

"I...I don't know if I can do this."

"But you will," the man replied. "I'm sure of it."

A troubling, lightheaded sensation overcame Gunari as he suddenly struggled to keep his balance on shaky legs. But the more he thought about replacing his old, crippled horse with a Gypsy Vanner, combined with the benefits of modern tools to quicken his repair work, the more this man's proposal intrigued him. Despite attempting something so dangerous and unpleasant, he decided then and there that his livelihood and family, his growing family, outweighed everything else.

"All right," he said. "I'll do it."

The man smiled again, unnerving Gunari in an unexplainable manner and forcing him to look away—something he felt unable to do moments before.

"Very good," the man said. "I knew you'd come to your senses. In three days, on Thursday afternoon, the mother will come to the market with her baby. Get there at three o'clock and wait. Be patient, she'll come."

The man reached into his pocket.

"Here's a photograph of her pushing the baby stroller, a distinctive, black-hooded type, so there will be no mistaking the target. The mother's face is clear to see, so you'll know exactly who to look for."

"How do you know she'll be there on Thursday?" Gunari asked. "And after three?"

"I just know," the man answered.

Standing several inches taller than Gunari's five-foot, nine-inch frame, the man glared down, his face no more than a foot away and commanding the Romani's complete attention.

"It must be this boy," he said, pointing his finger at the stroller. "Understand me, Gunari. This is the one I want."

***

Although the cooling temperature of this Bucharestian October day required sweaters or jackets of the passersby, trickles of sweat formed beneath the bill of Gunari's flat wool cap. Discarding his usual broad-brimmed hat, a requirement for his Vlach Romani attire, he wanted to avoid any cultural attention grabber. Wiping the drops away with the sleeve of his overcoat, he gazed in uncertainty at the lower portion of his disguise. The modern-day tapered pants, tucked into ill-fitting boots that squeezed his feet, replaced his usual baggy-styled black pants and black closed shoes. Another clothing obligation, his waistcoat with silver buttons, also remained a purposefully missing connection. Although he continued to rationalize the importance of doing this, the reality of the moment made him question his readiness.

The market stall stood in a thinly populated section of the north side, where the asphalt streets and final row of buildings led to a patchwork combination of cobblestone pathways and narrow, unpaved roads. At the end of those roads, about a four-to-five-minute walk from the market, a long row of uneven green shrubs ranging in height from seven to ten feet blocked the view of the large dirt field beyond. It was there, in those fields, on the outskirts of town, where Gunari lived with his wife in their vardo, his wagon, alongside the others of his Vlach Romani clan. Looking ahead to the short time remaining until his wife delivered their first child — the first of several they wanted, he believed his livelihood and the future of his family depended on the next few minutes. The disastrous consequences of getting caught were something he couldn't stop thinking about, like continuing to hear the rattling of bolted doors and windows during a howling windstorm.

Watching the mother approaching the market with the baby sitting up in a hooded black stroller, accompanied by another woman pushing hers in a dark blue pram, Gunari overheard their conversation, discovering that the name of his intended target was Petre. From his two previous days of observation, all the women who brought their babies here left them halfway in and side by side at the far right-hand section of the tent entrance. Gunari anticipated these women following the same routine, which they ultimately did, before walking together toward the last stall located on the opposite end. That section contained the more expensive food items, unaffordable for his people.

He didn't care for any of these women or their babies. They weren't Romani like him; they were gorgios, a term the Romani used to label anyone not of their kind. Gorgios looked down on his people, referring to them with the derogatory term "Gypsies" and believing they were nothing more than thieves and lazy beggars. Although most of the Romani males worked in respected occupations such as blacksmiths, farm laborers, horse traders, musicians, and his own specialty, cobbling shoes, the suspicious looks, and disrespectful treatment they continued to receive motivated him and steeled his conviction.

The market's location offered a stark contrast to the crowds and activity of Bucharest's main thoroughfare about a half mile away. Although this lessened the chance of being spotted, even if successful, the possibility remained that the mother might hear the baby cry as he fled. Still, the alternative of just grabbing the infant from the stroller seemed like a more dangerous option. Knowing he'd need to lift the baby into his arms in a rushed and ungentle manner seemed like an open invitation for sudden wailing.

And getting caught.

To avoid capture if seen escaping, Gunari accepted the possibility of abandoning the baby and running back toward the darkened alleyway that veered to the right between the last two buildings on the street. The similar heights of both structures blocked out any sunlight there, even in summer. The alley's back end led to the final group of hedges and the walking path leading to the Romani encampment several minutes away. The opposite side of the field, behind the living area, led to the larger trail for their wagons to come and go.

Taking his first step forward, he halted as the women stopped to chat with Simza, the talkative, gray-haired, mustachioed owner of the store.

"Shut up, Simza," he muttered.

In another two, maybe three minutes, they resumed their stroll, further distancing themselves from their babies in the extended enclosure. Although Simza supplied enough illumination under the tent to provide sufficient visibility, the increasing cloud layer, coupled with the late afternoon's naturally diminishing light, produced no better than a fuzzy clarity along the periphery. Gunari counted on this to help him remain as inconspicuous as possible.

Creeping closer, Gunari took advantage of the near blackness provided by a large adjacent awning as he darted to a spot behind a horse-drawn carriage tied to a signpost. No more than fifteen feet separated him from the babies, with Petre's stroller the closer of the two—an advantage, knowing, as he did, that every second counted. Taking one more look at the women's location, he hesitated again as another woman exited the market, waving goodbye to Simza and laughing at something he said before stopping to look and make stupid sounds at the babies.

As she walked away, Gunari closed his eyes and whispered a prayer. "I ask your help, God. I'm doing it for my family. I hope you understand and forgive me."

It was time.

Adrenaline surging, Gunari moved at a rapid pace toward the stroller, but he didn't run for fear of drawing attention to himself. Keeping his eyes focused on the two preoccupied women discussing a food item with Simza, Gunari placed his hand around the steel handle and maneuvered the carriage in a half circle. Without looking back, he broke into a fast walk toward the invisibility of another awning's extended shadow.

Scanning his surroundings and listening for screams from behind, the nervous anticipation of hearing something drove him to increase his speed, with each second bringing him closer to destination or capture. Reaching the shrubbery leading to the walking path where his sister, Lavinia, waited, his heartbeat slowed, his breathing deepened, and the determination to complete the mission strengthened his resolve.

The baby's muted cries, starting before Gunari reached the alleyway, signaled his awakening and an impending need for feeding. He had foreseen this possibility, and Lavinia, her breasts still full with a newborn of her own, offered them in advance upon his return. Nobody else knew of the theft, not even his wife, for fear of upsetting her so close to giving birth—and the unwanted persuasiveness of likely disapproval. His sister refused to hear any of the details of the plan and provided no encouragement for the idea, but knowing that her brother needed a new horse to maintain his business, had convinced Lavinia to help.

The quiet of the empty field brought the soft, musical jangling of the miniature yellow and gold bells hanging from Lavinia's left ear, announcing her approaching arrival. Reaching the stroller and peering down at the baby, Lavinia's eyes widened in a simultaneous drawing in of a sudden, quick breath.

"Gunari," she said, through an alarmed breathiness he resented, "what have you done?"

"What do you mean, what have I done?" he snapped, his head jerking back in confusion. "Exactly what I said I would do."

The increased crying from the awake and hungry baby irritated Gunari further, and when he leaned down to lift him, Lavinia nudged him away, giving her own baby to him and bringing the crying one to her chest.

"I'll feed the baby, but then we must return him immediately."

"What?" Gunari roared. "Are you crazy? This kid is going to make me enough money to buy that Gypsy Vanner. And new tools, too. I thought you understood that."

"I did," she replied, "but I didn't expect you to bring Petre."

Gunari's eyes narrowed in confusion as he stared at Lavinia.

"How do you know his name?"

Bouncing the baby in her arms, Lavinia looked down at his tiny face.

"His mother is Naomi, our midwife," she explained. "She's delivered every baby here since the time we arrived." Nodding her chin upward toward her own baby, she added, "Including my little Manfri!"

"But how do you know it's hers?" he asked. "This... this Naomi. There must be a lot of babies that look like him."

Lavinia shook her head.

"No, Gunari, it's not the baby that lets me know," she said, annoyance in her voice. "It's the blanket he's wrapped in. Look."

Lavinia held out the baby toward her brother.

"Naomi made this blanket. You can see it's handmade in the colors of the Romanian flag. When she was pregnant, she still came to deliver our babies, and she told us she was making one exactly like this—a blue, yellow, and red crotched blanket. So this must be it. It has to be. This little one is the midwife's baby, and we must bring him back to her."

An immediate surge of heat spread from Gunari's forehead down across his eyes, causing them to sting and moisten. This couldn't be happening. The cries from the baby increased in volume. Turning away from Gunari, Lavinia took several steps down the path before undoing her vest, unbuttoning her silk blouse, and suckling the baby.

"And if I don't agree to what you say, then what?" he asked, struggling to sound defiant despite a growing sense of doubt.

"You might not be wanted here anymore," Lavinia answered. "Our voivode, Motshan, may tell you to leave. He is our leader, and we listen to him. Naomi is a gorgio, but she is respected and appreciated for what she's done for us." Keeping her back to him, Lavina turned her head to look at her brother. "And it's not just the women who feel that way."

Gunari lowered his head for several moments, feeling a strangling sense of defeat. Motshan, the clan's chieftain, might do as Lavinia warned, especially if Gunari's actions led to further tension between the Romani and the citizens of Bucharest. If that happened, everyone's livelihood could be affected. He straightened and took a deep breath, pondering the inescapable irony of the darkening gray clouds bringing the curtain down on the fragmented remnants of blue.

"I have a plan that I hope will make this right," Lavinia said, the baby's mouth still attached to her nipple, "but I need you to hurry and put your Romani clothes back on. Naomi must be going crazy. We'll tell her we found him in the alley, and I recognized the carriage. We'll look like a couple of good Gypsies returning her baby but don't know anything else."

From a concealed area buried under fallen leaves at the base of a nearby oak tree, Gunari retrieved the bag of the discarded clothes he had removed earlier: the wide-brimmed hat, the dark overcoat, the waistcoat with silver buttons, and the loose-fitting black pants. With the extended, low-lying canopy providing the cover he required to change, they departed within a few minutes and headed back toward the market.

Not more than thirty seconds after reappearing from the alleyway, they first heard a woman scream, "Petre!" before seeing Naomi rushing toward them, her arms outstretched in a frantic gesture of need. Grabbing the baby and sweeping him into her arms before clutching him to her chest, Naomi's sobs continued to fill the air as she turned and walked away, distancing herself from the two of them. When Simza and the other woman with the pram approached and viewed the scene, they both leered at Gunari and Lavinia before heading toward Naomi, each placing a hand on a separate shoulder. Simza whispered something before turning around and, with a stiff and accusatory gait, moved in like a policeman to pull the carriage away.

"Cum indraznesti," he muttered, telling them, "How dare you," through teeth clenched in disgust.

Grabbing Lavinia's arm, Gunari said, "Let's get out of here. It's not safe."

Lavinia's dark eyes flashed revulsion at her brother. Defiant and angry, she held Manfri in one arm and pulled away from his grip with the other. She approached Naomi, one cautious step followed by another leading her to within ten feet of the midwife.

"Naomi," she said, her voice cracking, "it's me, Lavinia. I'm so sorry this happened to you. We...we were in the field when we heard the baby crying. He was in the alley back there."

"You're lying!" Naomi's friend shouted. "And you should leave now."

Simza stared at Lavinia in silence, but his hateful expression caused her to question their safety, just as Gunari feared. Walking away and eager to leave, she heard Naomi's voice.

"Wait."

Lavinia glanced at Gunari before turning around. Naomi approached her, staring through brown eyes markedly bloodshot and puffy. Disheveled strands of her neck-length auburn hair hung limp and sticky from underneath her headscarf.

"I remember you, Lavinia," she said, her voice hoarse but clear. "How's your baby? Manfri is his name, right?"

Lavinia smiled. "Yes," she answered, looking down at him. "He's doing fine, thank you."

Naomi took a deep breath, her stare remaining unmoving as a spotlight.

"I don't know what happened, and I'm not going to go to the police," she said. "Many of you are good people, and you've been kind to me. The women I've met…I saw their babies take their first breath…I know what will happen to all of you if the police come, and I don't want to bring that kind of trouble."

Wrapping her arms in a tighter embrace around Petre, she lowered her face and kissed the child before continuing. "I'm quite aware of the persecution the Romani face here. I see it on the streets and in the shops. I hear it in the things people say, even those I know and consider my friends. But I'll tell you something else, Lavinia. We Romanian Jews also know persecution. We also understand what it's like to be hated, to feel unwelcome, to be looked upon as people who can't be trusted."

Wiping away a tear, she gazed outward again toward Gunari, holding his gaze for several moments before looking back at Lavinia and offering a sad smile.

"My last name is Levy," she said, "a very Jewish name. In Romania, right here in Bucharest, that's caused a lot of problems for my husband and me. What happened today has nothing to do with being Jewish, but I see it as an omen. We had already decided to leave Romania to join my sister and her family. And now, after what happened to my baby, it can't come soon enough."

Furrowing her eyebrows, Lavinia asked, "Where are you going?"

"Far away from here," Naomi answered. "To America."

CHAPTER TWO
A PROCLAMATION AND A VOW

Zigzagging his way through grassy brush and a predominant mix of pine and black locust trees, Gunari hurried to the designated location in the Băneasa Forest, dreading the thought of showing up empty-handed. His anxiety over failing to deliver the baby intensified with the stranger's sudden appearance from a veiled area, startling Gunari and causing him to jerk back in surprise with another ten minutes distance remaining to reach the arranged site.

Observing the man's angry expression—or who he thought might be the same man—Gunari's heartbeat accelerated, and his breath grew short. On the cusp of the disappearing daylight within the wooded curtain of trees, Gunari still retained a clear enough view of the man's face, confusing him at the unsettling change in his appearance. His bald head and lack of eyebrows contrasted with the bushy black hair in both locations from the day they met. His mouth seemed wider, his lips more pronounced, and the seemingly whiter skin enhanced shadowy circles under his eyes that must have escaped his notice before. Even his voice seemed different, deeper. Yet even with these changes, Gunari concluded that this man was, indeed, the same person.

Dressing in black from top to bottom and blending further into the sunless forest with each darkening minute, it struck Gunari that the man appeared closer to a floating head than an entire person. Feeling mesmerized by a peculiar glow emanating from those coal-colored eyes, Gunari's sudden and unexplainable limitation on his ability to speak baffled and disturbed him. Standing in silent obeyance, he listened.

"You have failed me, Gunari," the man said, his words uttered in slow, simmering condemnation. "Will my plans for that boy no longer come to pass? Am I now unable to show him the way? Who I am? What I am? And what he should be a part of?"

A drawn-out shaking of his head followed.

"For this, you must pay a price," he exclaimed, the power of his stare staggering Gunari. "But first, you must explain yourself."

Inhaling several large gulps of air as if released from the gagging of his mouth, Gunari found his voice again.

"What do you mean I must pay a price?" he asked. "This wasn't my fault. My plan worked, and I got you what you wanted. But how was I to know the baby belonged to…"

"Enough!" the man shouted. Hands emerging from the blackness suddenly materialized under his chin, with one cupped around the other as his eyes continued to hold Gunari in their grasp. Despite the normally refreshing, cool air of dusk, Gunari felt lead-footed and fatigued. Rubbing a hand across his face, he waited, a dire recognition of helplessness overtaking him. As if struck by a whip, the man's next few words sent a surge of panic coursing through his entire being.

"Your wife is expecting soon, Gunari?"

"Yes, and you stay away!" he shouted, jolted from the shackles of his deference.

Gunari's body stiffened, preparing to defend himself after his outburst.

"I had bigger and better plans," the man said. "And it started with that Jewish baby."

"Why?" Gunari asked. "What did you want to do? And why did he have to be Jewish?"

The man paused, his lips curling into a snarl, exposing teeth the same yellowish tinge of the bowls cradling his black eyes — another physical change from their first meeting.

"I will answer you," he said, "and when I'm finished, you will understand the consequences of your failure."

Closing his eyes for a moment, in the next instant, he opened them wide, a surge of intensity making Gunari feel as if a hole bore through his skull.

"I, and all who are like me, date back to the early days of man," he explained. "We're the product of seeds born from his dark side, blooming and proliferating and as natural as the mountains and forests around us. But our inception didn't originate like you, from copulation and procreation. No, our beginnings can be traced to the time when thought and imagination started veering from the path the Creator intended, leading toward the corruption of the soul. Spreading like a contagious disease. Infecting humanity with multiple viruses of our making. And as the world's population grew, so did we, the driving force behind man's continual inhumanity to man. Natural and earthborn, yes, but nature-altered. Nature dedicated for a different purpose."

Gunari shook his head in disbelief.

"I don't know what you're talking about," he said. "You must be out of your mind. I just thought you were someone wanting to give me money to buy a horse in exchange for a baby. Who are you, anyway?"

The man responded with a sinister-sounding chuckle.

"Many people call me the Devil," he said, his voice sounding calm and assured. "But that's just a name. Just a word. And those people have it all wrong. They think there's just one Devil because they believe in their one God. They think I act alone, that every type of evil in this world is because of one single entity. But why does it have to be one versus one? I don't know who determined those rules, but it's far from the truth. There are many of us, evolved and connected like branches from the same tree."

Lowering his voice to a raspy whisper, he added, "And we're everywhere."

With a tongue now devoid of moisture, Gunari licked his lips as he felt trickles of sweat forming on the back of his neck and under his hat.

"That's...crazy talk," he said. "You're crazy."

Ignoring Gunari's remark, the man continued.

"Sometimes we strike when something is new, like when a life is just beginning. The goodness intended at birth no longer matters to us. It's too late for that. We're now in a constant state of war with God, whatever your beliefs and whatever name is given. As God is the foundation of faith, we rationalize and inspire uncertainty. As God is the basis of your belief, we instill doubt. As God is your motivation for hope, we give ample reason for hopelessness. The manipulation of humans is so easy. Sometimes, too easy. It's a war for the soul, and we strike when the moment is right. Either way, we seek to achieve what we were meant to do. Man's inhumanity to man is simply us doing our job, as you might say."

Gritting his teeth and struggling to find the right words, Gunari became determined to show the strength of his faith against such insanity. "I'm a good Christian man," he said, "and your words make you sound like someone who needs God's help."

Deep-throated laughter bellowed forth from the man, shredding Gunari's attempt at bravery.

"No, no, no, it's God who needs help, not me. No matter which God is referred to, there's something every religion needs to admit. For a long, long time now, God has been unable to keep up with humanity's constant dependence. Their continual needs. Simply put, God is overwhelmed."

The man chuckled.

"How do you think I got here?" he asked. "How did an evil like me evolve from God's so-called perfection?"

Leering at Gunari, he proceeded to answer his own question. "None of us individually have the strength to compete against God, but just like packs of animals can bring down a larger, stronger one, we intend to do the same."

"That can never happen," Gunari said. "God protects us all."

"All of you?" the man asked, still chuckling. "History disagrees, Gunari, and I can go on for days with example after example. Those like me started multiplying in this world while God's attention focused on too many other things that you humans brought to bear upon yourselves. That gave us the opening we needed, and thanks to the frailties of human nature as we envisioned it, the evil we bring continues to spread throughout the world."

Nodding his head in a slow up and down motion, the man spoke with a self-assured calm.

"We are becoming that pack of animals."

Gunari shook his head in furious denial. "Do you think I believe any of this?" he growled, his parched throat betraying the emotion he wanted to convey. "Who are you, really?"

"Do I look different to you, Gunari?" he asked. "Are you thinking I've possibly changed from the day we met?"

Taken aback by the acknowledgment of something he'd observed from the beginning, Gunari peered at the man, nodding several times.

"It's not your imagination," he said. "There are many living things that shed their skin, but I'm shedding my host, my dying spirit. The time is coming when I'll move on to the body of another. And when that happens, when I require sustenance, as I often do," a small smile appeared, "I will feed on flesh and blood and bone."

Gunari felt a sudden chill, unsure whether the shaking in his body derived from the cooling temperature, fear, or both. Crossing his heart, he tried to steady himself.

"That baby…what were you going to do with it?" he asked.

"I now desire a new host, and he was my choice."

"But…why a Jewish baby? I don't understand."

"Call it my contribution to the future," the man replied. "In a relatively short period of time, Germany will have a powerful leader whose impact will affect the entire world. He'll be one of our greatest creations, and his name and influence will survive long after his death. That man's soul is now inhabited by one of us, transformed into an instrument for evil beyond anything you could imagine. This man will cause the suffering and eradication of millions of Jews. Millions, Gunari. And here in Romania, another host, another altered soul, will become this country's leader, causing many more thousands of Jews to die under his watch. Belief in a God is the driving force behind all major religions, but if that belief can be destroyed by enough acts of evil, faith shrivels up and crumbles like a dead leaf."

The man paused, his tight, pale lips forming a slight smile.

"The way I see it," he said, "I'd be doing that Jewish baby a favor by seizing his soul before he's old enough to suffer a grievous loss of faith at what's to come."

Clenching his fists, Gunari pursed his lips, shaking his head in a deliberate back and forth response several times.

"A loss of faith because of that German leader or because you stole that baby's soul?" he asked, his tone angry and accusatory. "How do you know what he'll believe in? What he'll think? How he'll react? Every one of those millions of deaths will be your fault. But it's not too late to change it. It doesn't have to be that way."

His eyes narrowing, the man stared at Gunari for several moments before responding.

"Remember who we are," he said. "We have no

sympathy for the Jewish people, the Romani people, or anyone else. Every war, every torture, every rape, every enslavement, every famine, every form of human abuse, they all have our mark. They're all guided by our ideas and desires. That Jewish baby is only one soul, but there will be hundreds, thousands, millions more to invade and conquer. How do I know this? Because we're immortal, Gunari. Wherever human suffering exists, and it will continue to exist everywhere, we will always be there, the puppet masters of chaos and misery."

His head spinning from so much talk and so many schemes he didn't understand, Gunari's thoughts turned to his people. After centuries of persecution, would they suffer more?

"And the Romanis?" he asked. "What about us? What will be our fate?"

"Like the Jews, your people will be seen as an impure race to be eliminated," he answered. "And others, too. You will all suffer the consequences of pure hatred."

"No," he cried. "We're good people. All we want is to live in peace."

The man's response, spoken in a serene, unhurried demeanor, caused Gunari to weaken and grow disoriented.

"Good people become irrelevant," the man said. "As long as we're around."

Gunari hurried a hand across watering eyes, his frightful thoughts the useful equivalent of a well gone dry.

"I never did anything to you," he said. "Leave me and my family alone."

The man scowled, bloodshot eyes enhancing his menacing expression.

"I don't accept defeat easily," he replied. "Had you delivered that baby to me, he was to become part of my realm, a part of my future. Our future. Together. And with that union, his mother's spirit in the afterlife would be destined to wander a loveless void of separation, left without any spiritual connection to her son. No divine encounter. No eternal peace."

Drops of perspiration started rolling freely down Gunari's forehead and under his arms.

"Nobody can do what you're saying," Gunari replied. "I wish I'd never met you. You're insane."

"Look at me," he said. "I'm sensing a change in fortune. Look into my eyes."

Wiping away a tear, Gunari closed his eyes in defiance.

"Look at me, Gunari!" the man commanded, his voice raising.

Taking several rapid breaths, his chest heaving in preparation, Gunari gathered the courage to gaze again into those mysterious, unsettling eyes. This time, however, he discerned a heightened danger and started swaying on immovable legs, unable to turn away or look in a different direction.

"I want you to picture the baby's face in your mind," the man told him.

"I...I don't understand."

"Think, think hard about the baby's face. What did he look like?"

Gunari licked his parched lips and swallowed, his burning throat rebelling against the lack of any saliva. Despite not having the time to focus on the baby's features as he hurried from the market, he did get the chance for a good view during his moments with Lavinia.

"I remember the eyes the most," Gunari said. "They were round and kind of large for a baby. And they were blue, I'm sure of that. Not a lot of hair yet, but enough to cover his head. It was a dark brown color and straight, not curly. It fell over the top of his forehead a little. And his forehead looked kind of big to me. He had a round face, big cheeks, and his ears stuck out at the tips a little. Not a lot, but enough for me to notice. The nose seemed kind of round at the tip, not pointy. Nothing about the mouth really stood out. Just a normal-looking mouth. That's...that's the best I can tell you."

Apparently, whatever facial recollection Gunari etched in his mind did more than just satisfy the man's request. Baring his teeth, a wicked smile spread on his face, culminating in a delirious look of madness. Within moments, the smile evolved into abbreviated, barking laughs before escalating into a maniacal-sounding howl.

"You didn't deliver that baby to me, but he'll still be mine," the man said, still reacting with a feverish glee. "I see him through your eyes, straight to the memory inside your mind. And I'm witnessing something that delights me." With his gaze burrowing deeper into what felt like a possession of Gunari himself, he continued. "I see him as a young man. A strong young man who will die a violent death here in Romania, his home country." In a sudden whisper, chilling Gunari's blood, the man added, "And that death will bring him back to me."

Silence ensued for several seconds until a crow cawed from somewhere in the forest.

"And so, my proclamation is this: When the mother dies in the years following her son's death and returns as a reborn spirit, she will seek the holy union of life and death with him. But she'll find he's no longer there. The mother will remain forever separated, forever wandering, never resting in peace without her son."

Gunari grew short of breath, listening in fear but not quite comprehending.

"And the son?" he asked, his voice soft and hesitant. "What happens to him after he dies?"

The surrounding oily tinges of red and yellow framing the man's black orbs seemed to enhance the narcotic-like effect holding Gunari prisoner as he listened to the answer.

"The son's reawakening shall commence exactly seventy-four years from the day of his death. Seventy-four years, an entirely appropriate time." Rubbing his hands together, he explained further. "In Jewish mysticism, the number seventy-four represents the absence of light or, as I prefer to say, the emergence of darkness. How perfectly fitting that it will be the emergence of him and me, of our darkness, together as one. His body will be my vessel, and his spirit will live through me. I will control that vessel, Gunari. I will be the captain of that ship."

"I don't understand," Gunari said. "If you wanted him as a healthy baby, why would you still want him years later when he's dead?"

"That's an easy question to answer," the man told him. "It's not just a human feature to believe in fate. We find it as mysterious as you do and something not to be discounted. I wanted to turn that baby's soul into my own creation. Thanks to your negligence and your inexcusable carelessness, I'm unable to do so. But knowing he will return and die here, as is his fate, I now plan to occupy his eternal spirit to use as another means for my intended purposes."

Gunari placed his hand over his mouth, holding it there as he tried to steady himself, anxious for this unnerving conversation to end. The usual aromatic autumn air of the forest now seemed stale, leaving an unpleasant odor of decay he couldn't pinpoint.

"You failed to bring the baby to me," the man said, his tone threatening. "And even though his spirit will one day be mine, you have forced me to alter my plans, to wait."

"I know," he said, his voice low and shaky. "I'm sorry."

"Apologies are like dust," he snarled. "Nothing but words that float and linger until they choke someone on their uselessness."

Gunari watched as the man's figure started fading into the darkness of the forest, leaving him hearing words seemingly spoken from out of nowhere.

"Your time has come, Gunari."

A whooshing sound followed by crunching leaves snapped Gunari out of whatever spell had prevented him from turning away. Rushing toward the area of trees where the man first appeared, he saw and heard nothing more through the darkness. He stood there for an indeterminate amount of time, reflecting on his encounter and feeling confused over what had transpired. Inhaling deep, restorative breaths of the gratifying, cool, woodsy air, he felt calmer as he began regaining his clear-headedness. Concluding that the man must have possessed the ability of trickery, perhaps as a hypnotist or maybe an illusionist, Gunari headed back toward the campsite, now convinced that the hate-filled language and nightmarish prophecy represented nothing more than the words of a madman. Anxious to be with his pregnant wife, he started devising a story to explain his absence. That story, however, wouldn't be necessary.

In the chilly, early morning drizzle the following day, when enough light allowed a search party to look for Gunari Boswell, they found his pale, bloodied, and partially devoured body about a half-mile inside the nearby Băneasa Forest. Despite the rarity of a wolf attacking a human, the mutilated flesh, a head-to-toe abomination, appeared to be from the claws and teeth of a wild animal, perhaps more than one, and many gray wolves resided in the forests of Romania. Whatever the cause, no one understood his reason for venturing deep into the forest, especially after sunset.

Two months later, with the aid of a new midwife from town, his wife gave birth to a boy she named Gunari.

Twenty-three years later, under the dictatorship of Romania's Ion Antonescu, the young Gunari and his mother came to be two of approximately nineteen thousand murdered Romani in that country during World War II and two of several hundred thousand throughout Europe under the Axis coalition.

***

Hearing the soft knock, Naomi leaned down to lift a cranky Petre into her arms before opening the door. Unsurprisingly, she found herself looking into the familiar brown eyes of the Romani's phuri dai, Ivona, the senior woman of the clan, who oversaw the activities of the women and children. Naomi's relationship with Ivona started from the first Romani baby she assisted in delivering after their arrival on the outskirts of the city. Dressed in a long, maroon-colored skirt with a flowery charcoal-gray blouse, gold necklaces and bracelets, and a multicolored headscarf called a Diklo, her attire represented the traditional clothing of the Vlach Romani women.

With the horrible incident from the day before continuing to leave her emotions raw and fragile, Naomi figured that the sorrowful look on Ivona's face foretold the reason for her visit—to offer comfort and support. Entering the small, two-bedroom home, Ivona refused Naomi's offer to sit, electing to stand near the door. A large, heavyset woman of above average height, Ivona stood close to the five-foot, four-inch Naomi and looked downward to stare into her eyes.

"Naomi," she said, shaking her head, "I speak for all the Romani women when I say I'm so sorry about what happened yesterday. Although you are not one of us, you are held in very high esteem. I hope you know that."

Naomi bounced Petre in a gentle up-and-down manner, trying to calm him.

"Thank you, Ivona," she replied. Gazing at her baby, Naomi's eyes filled with tears. "I was so afraid I lost him."

"Bunica Sofia is asking to see you," Ivona said. "And your baby, too. She's outside in our vardo."

Naomi's head reared back in surprise at the news that the revered and mystical woman known to all as Bunica Sofia, Grandma Sofia, not only wanted to talk with her but waited in a wagon at that moment. Though they'd never met, Naomi spent enough time with the Romani women to have heard stories of her allegedly accurate predictions about things concerning births, deaths, travels, and dangers. Naomi remained skeptical, sharing those doubts with her husband but nobody else.

Placing Petre in the black stroller, Naomi followed Ivona as she wheeled the whimpering baby toward the wagon—stopping when another Romani woman looked at her, held up a hand, and turned away to speak to someone inside. Petre's crankiness lingered, the restive mood continuing from early that morning.

"Stay here," Ivona said, standing by the large, gold-painted, wood-rimmed wheels. "I'll see if Bunica Sofia is ready."

Although having no legitimate reason to feel anxious about meeting the woman, Naomi's heart started beating faster, and she felt her face flush. Perhaps the anticipation of finally meeting the mysterious Bunica Sofia was affecting her, and Petre's fussy mood didn't help. Blowing out a gust of deeply inhaled air, she waited.

When Ivona waved her over, the other woman placed a small stepladder at the base of the interior entrance so she could climb inside.

"I'll hand your baby to you," Ivona said, "and then the carriage."

Ascending the ladder, Naomi first observed the ornate interior, scanning the ivory-and-gold-flowered wallpaper working in harmony with the white, lacy window curtains. Looking up, she surveyed the gold beads and coin necklaces dangling from the ceiling and, on the floor, the intricate black, red, and green colored throw rug. She smiled in appreciation at the finely carved wood beams and the desk with gold candlesticks. The windowless wall on the left held three wood-framed circular mirrors, and the bed consisted of a gold-colored mattress with ivory-colored cushions on a shiny, cherrywood frame. She then directed her attention to the back of Bunica Sofia, sitting in a wheelchair facing the bed. The woman didn't move or say a word when Naomi entered, remaining that way until she held Petre in her arms and the carriage handle in her hand.

"Bring your baby to me," she said, her voice carrying with enough strength to still be heard despite facing in the other direction.

Naomi resumed her attempts to calm Petre as she walked past the chair and sat on the bed. Gazing at the diminutive woman with snow-colored hair cascading down her back like a river-swollen waterfall, Naomi appreciated the fashionable attire worn by this leather-jacketed figure in her multicolored shawl and ankle-length, forest-green skirt.

Possessing a face that appeared simultaneously ancient and youthful, depending on where one looked, Bunica Sofia's delicate, smooth, white cheeks and broad, lineless forehead belied the thin, colorless lips and eyelid-enshrouded pale blue eyes that continued providing the frail woman just enough ability to see, judging by their shifting movement from Naomi to Petre. Lifting her bony left hand toward the baby, exposing four stiffened, bent fingers and a completely curled inward forefinger, she nodded her head and blinked several times, making the murky remnants of her eye resemble a frosty afternoon shadow.

"Hand him to me."

"I'm sorry about his crying," Naomi said, leaning forward. "He's having a bad day."

Extending her arms, she laid the baby on Bunica Sofia's lap, keeping her hands close. In a slow, methodical motion, the old woman placed her own hand on Petre's head and, to Naomi's surprise, started singing a familiar Romanian lullaby, "Cantec De Leagan." Concluding the first verse and continuing into the second, she swept her palm in gentle, back-and-forth strokes across the top of the baby's forehead. As Naomi watched, amazed at the strength of Bunica Sofia's voice, the crying began to subside, first in volume and then in consistency. Within a short amount of time, perhaps a little more than three minutes, the soft breathing from the sleeping baby dominated the sound in the room.

"Now place him in his carriage," Bunica Sofia said. "We must talk."

Naomi did as requested, then returned to her previous spot and sat, curious to know the reason for this meeting. Bunica Sofia first looked toward the floor as if in deep thought. Raising and lowering her bony shoulders with a quiet breath, she lifted her head to look into Naomi's eyes.

"You are a gorgio, an outsider to our people, yet you have helped us bring new Romani lives into this world. I am an old woman who has seen much and will soon be gone." She smiled, transforming her smooth yet thin skin into a sudden intersection of wrinkles from her cheeks to her temples. "You have earned the right to know what I must tell you before I am no longer here."

"Tell me what?" Naomi asked. "Is this about what happened yesterday?"

Bunica Sofia closed her eyes and nodded, the slight motion of her head difficult to detect at first.

"Yes," she replied. "But not about somebody taking your baby. There's more you need to know."

"What do you mean?" Naomi said.

"I sensed a very strong disturbance," Bunica Sofia told her. "Something evil. But I come here to offer you reassurance."

Sitting in silence, Naomi didn't know what to make of this odd and aged woman speaking about scary things, and she reminded herself that those stories of prophecies coming true seemed like silly exaggerations. Concluding that there wasn't anything worth responding to and knowing she was leaving Bucharest for the faraway land of America anyway, she smiled and offered a gentle pat on the woman's leg.

"Thank you for coming, Bunica Sofia, and I'll remember what you said about the reassurance. But I should be getting Petre back to finish his nap."

"Wait," she said, holding up a hand, its wrinkled steadiness repudiating her age. "I have one more thing you need to hear. It's the reason I came to talk with you, and it does concern your baby."

Gripping her thighs, Naomi asked, "Is Petre safe? Please tell me that he'll be safe."

With her body remaining fixed to the chair, Bunica Sofia brought her head forward and stared into Naomi's eyes.

"Hear me out, dear one," she said. "We Romani believe that when a bird flies into one's home, it's a sign of death." She pointed her bent fingers toward the window on the opposite side from the mirrors. "See that window?" she asked. "This morning, it was open, and a crow landed on the ledge. It wasn't here long, and it flew out where you entered." Bunica Sofia turned her head in that direction long enough to take a deep breath and pause for a moment. "I tell you this because I now believe my life is nearing an end, and my prophecy to you shall be my last." Looking at the arched wood beams above her, or perhaps the gaze was intended instead for the sky beyond, she continued. "Your son will be taken from you two more times."

"What?" Naomi cried. "What are you saying? How do you know this? Will it be one of your people?"

"No," Bunica Sofia answered. "Not one of my people. I promise you that." Placing her hand on Naomi's knee, she leaned forward and said, "Please let me finish."

Shaken, Naomi said, "All right, go ahead. I'm listening."

Bunica Sofia nodded her head and removed her hand from Naomi's knee to resume her previous position in the chair.

"There are spiritual beliefs, good and bad, about prophecy givers like me who reach one hundred years of age," she told her. "My abilities are altering, rearranging themselves into a final phase of power and foresight. The disturbance I experienced yesterday, that...evil, created my need to meet with you and take you into my soul's passageway so that I may help you when that time arrives."

Bunica Sofia extended her frail arm toward Naomi.

"Give me your hand," she said.

In a slow, unsure gesture, Naomi reached out and did as requested.

"Today, I vow my connection to your life force, which shall continue even in death. And in the world of your afterlife, although you may feel disconnected and unsettled from the power of an unholy source, you can still defeat that evil. We can defeat that evil. We must. And when that is done, when that immoral compass leading to destruction is a thing of the past, you will find your way back to reunite with your son in everlasting peace."

Abandoning her previous pessimism about this woman's reputation, the terrifying severity of the message frightened Naomi and brought her to the verge of tears. Rising from the edge of the bed and anxious to leave, she looked down into Bunica Sofia's timeworn eyes, feeling the need to ask a final question.

"And how will I defeat that evil?"

The old woman smiled, the fading remnants of the blue in those eyes seeming to intensify at that moment.

"Through the power of your message, my child. The power of your love."

***

With her white-knuckled grip clutching the carriage handle, Naomi's tears formed and fell as she returned home. With no intention of telling her husband, Stefan, already enraged about the day before, the thought of keeping such horrible things a secret left her drained. Petre separated from her two more times? How dare that woman scare her like that!

"A connection to my life force continuing in death?" Naomi said, speaking in a volume as if in conversation with someone in the room. "What's that supposed to mean, anyway? When she dies, and when I die, we'll both be in our graves, resting in peace."

CHAPTER THREE
RETURN TO ROMANIA

Benghazi, Libya, July 31, 1943

Colonel Jacob Smart commanded the complete attention of the packed room of United States airmen from the Eighth and Ninth Air Force as they listened to the final details of a daring and strategically crucial bombing raid planned for the next day, August 1. Comprising just three of the total number of bomb groups, the Eighth Air Force provided the vital addition of extra firepower from their heavy bomb payload — four tons of explosives. A member of the Eighth Air Force's 44th, Airman Peter Levy, leaned forward in a narrow, green metal folding chair, grasping his thighs with the sturdy grip of an experienced bomber's machine gun ready hands. His right leg pumping up and down in a piston-like simulation, Levy's nervous energy dictated the moment and exemplified the mood of everyone in attendance.

With the aid of a pointer and a movie screen in the semi-dark room, Smart highlighted the locations as he outlined the scope of the attack.

"At oh-three hundred hours, Operation Tidal Wave will commence. One hundred seventy-seven B-24 Liberator bombers will take off from the Benghazi airfields and fly northeast toward our target—the nine major oilfields of Ploesti, Romania." Rapping the tip of his pointer in a quick three-beat whack on Ploesti's location on the map, he paused while continuing to stare at the screen. "This damn city isn't called 'Hitler's Gas Station' for nothing, men. An estimated one third of all the oil used by Germany is produced here— that's over eight million tons of oil annually. So if we're successful, if we can bomb the hell out of those factories, it will be a big-time kick in the nuts to those Nazi assholes."

Loud clapping and whooping exploded from the room. Peter felt a slap on his shoulder, courtesy of his good friend, Alberto Lombardi, the bombardier in charge of making sure the accuracy of those 4,000 pounds landed squarely on their designated targets.

"Those bastards won't know what hit 'em, Pete," he said, his smile concealing his nervousness. "And when we get back, you're buying the first round."

Turning around, Peter looked at Alberto, his thick, dark brows highlighting a natural intensity to his penetrating, blue-eyed stare. Sliding a flat hand along his cropped brown hair, Peter responded with a quick upward thrust of his chin in acknowledgment.

"You're on, Lombardi," he said. "And we'll have more than one, brother."

A tense silence dominated the atmosphere once again as Smart resumed his speech.

"In June last year, we conducted a smaller operation

on this area, so you can bet your ass the Germans are much better prepared now. But that's only if their radar picks us up." With the pointer remaining in his hand, Smart took a couple of steps forward and faced the room. "Those low-level bombing exercises you've conducted in the African desert were designed to prepare you for tomorrow. Why? Because if we're going to be successful, we need to fly in undetected, under their radar, and not give their batteries a chance to get ready. That not only means radio silence the entire way but also no fighter support. There is no other option. That's the only way we're going to avoid their weapons and get to those refineries."

A noticeable murmur arose from the assembly with the news of a radio silence mission with no fighter support—a considerable ramping up of the danger level.

Before Smart returned to the map, Peter's eyes reached it ahead of him, surveying the flight routes over the Mediterranean and Adriatic Seas, crossing over the Pindus Mountains in Yugoslavia and then into the country of his birth, Romania. Taking a few seconds to add the distance in his head, he figured the mission totaled close to 2,000 miles. Subjects like math and geography formed and settled easily in his head due in no small part to his mother's attention on him and her emphasis on a good education. With the death in childbirth of his sister and his mother's inability to conceive again, his upbringing as an only child had created an environment of a united, three-member family until the tragic death of his father four years earlier of tuberculosis. It took going to war against Hitler's Germany and the other Axis powers to separate Peter from his remaining immediate family member, his mother, Naomi.

Concluding his talk and answering all questions, Smart sent the men back to their barracks for rest and, as he suggested, letter writing—an assignment everyone welcomed. As with any perilous mission, especially in the hard-to-maneuver B-24 Liberator bomber planes bleakly referred to as the Flying Coffin, the unspoken probability of more bombers leaving than returning remained not only high but probable. Letter writing took on a crucial importance.

Propped up against his pillow after changing into a dry T-shirt necessitated by the Libyan heat, Peter gazed around a silent room filled with tobacco smoke, tension, and fear. He observed men keeping busy with writing or reading. The ones Peter focused on the most, however, were those airmen lying flat and open-eyed, staring at the ceiling as they inhaled, like him, deep mouthfuls from their cigarettes. He didn't see anyone sleeping. Despite his past successes—and luck, always luck—flying previous missions as one of the two waist gunners standing by an open bay window, defending the plane's most vulnerable sides with nothing more than a .50 caliber machine gun brought a perilous and often fatal risk. Peter understood what every member of any military always knows—the next battle might be your dying day, and, in Peter's case, it would also be his twenty-third birthday. It was young men like him in their early twenties who comprised the majority of those who flew the air raids, and it saddened him to know that any of them, including him, might not live to see their mid-twenties.

Perhaps because of the untested task and inherent danger involved in Operation Tidal Wave, as well as the obvious need to maintain secrecy, Peter's letter to his mother focused on reminisces about his life back home — the holidays, family vacations, his friends, his school days, the sports he played, his favorite meals, his broken heart when his high school girlfriend moved away, and his even bigger broken heart when Samson died — their beloved white, black, and tan-colored Pug. After writing nonstop for three pages, he finished up with his thoughts about their family history:

...So that got me thinking about my life with my parents, the wonderful Steven and Naomi Levy. It's funny to me how my real name is Petre, and Dad's was Stefan. But as you've explained to me, those American guys at Ellis Island needed to keep it simple and American, and both of you welcomed the opportunity to assimilate from the start. But baby Petre was too young to understand and appreciate that arrival day in New York City. It took those first eight years in St. Louis and then our move to Boyle Heights in sunny Los Angeles to make me recognize how grateful I am for how things turned out.

I loved growing up there. What kid doesn't enjoy the chance to play outside and do sports all year round? The beach, the snow in the mountains, the desert, they all left me with great memories. And, of course, how could I not mention all those cute girls? Nothing against St. Louis, but when Dad's boss moved to Los Angeles to help construct the facilities for the Olympics, how fortunate it was that he invited Dad to also make the move with a guaranteed job and housing. Dad was a master electrician, and thank God he had the talent to stay employed and get us through the worst of the Depression.

And look at what you did, raising a rascal like me, giving us a happy home, and with all of that, getting your degree from the Jewish Hospital School of Nursing. Now you're working at Mt. Sinai Hospital and those patients are lucky as can be to have you caring for them.

Mom, I've said this before, but it bears repeating. You were always the rock of our family, and I've never known anyone stronger than you. You lost a baby, your sister's car accident left her paralyzed halfway across the country, and your husband died from tuberculosis. But when it comes to determination, to an absolute will to survive and carry on, your example has shown me the way and helped me get through some tough times during this war.

I hope you now realize there's nothing more you could have done to prevent Dad's death, just like so many others from that terrible disease. I know how much you tried, all those hours of research you put in, and all those difficult days and nights you cared for him. Dad's now resting in peace, no longer suffering, and is with our little Camellia at that beautiful gravesite in Evergreen Cemetery. Next time you visit, tell him that along with making the best barbequed ribs in the world and possessing a pretty decent hook shot, Peter says he was also the best dad a son could ever have, and I love him very much.

As I love you very much, Mom. Always.

Hope to see you again soon.

Peter

Perhaps some men managed a few hours of sleep that night, but Peter sensed an overall inability throughout the barracks. With each passing hour seeming interminably longer than the one before, he zeroed in on the lack of customary sleeping sounds, such as snoring or peaceful breathing patterns. The telltale sounds of restlessness, reflected by the constant stirring and occasional coughs, permeated the darkness. Peter conceded any sleep at all as an improbability. At some point before dawn, however, he did fall asleep — and when he awoke, shaken by the detailed recollection of his dream, he wished he hadn't slept at all. As the visibility of the ceiling started coming into view, Peter propped himself up in bed, still haunted by the images of his nightmare about the flight.

***

The tremoring body of the B-24 continued navigating deeper into the darkening, smoke-filled sky as the cacophony of exploding enemy bombs neared their target by ever decreasing distances. From the open window of his waist gunner position, Peter spotted a Messerschmitt fighter plane approaching from the east in a direct line toward where he stood. With his finger wrapped tightly around the trigger, Peter started spraying multiple rounds in rapid succession.

The plane kept coming, continuing its approach as if specifically zeroing in toward Peter himself, and as he watched the ineffectiveness of his bullets bounce off the all-metal body and window of the closed canopy, the German's plane angled away, disappearing for several seconds before coming back around into a sudden side-by-side position with the B-24. Staring in equal parts confusion and disbelief, Peter stopped firing and gaped into the cockpit at a helmetless, bald-headed man with black, maniacal eyes pointing at him and laughing. His demonic expression seemed almost inhuman, as something that can only be described as wolfish in appearance. Within moments, the Messerschmitt vanished, leaving no trace of its existence.

Peter remained immobile, shocked at witnessing the impossible. As the reality of the here and now returned to his consciousness, he turned around in terror as fire started spreading throughout the inside of the plane. Scrambling for his parachute, he heard the screams of his fellow airmen. Hurrying to ready his jacket for escape, with everything now in place to jump, he looked up and saw the others standing motionless together before him, without parachutes and their faces down, leaving Peter a view of nothing but the top of their headgear.

"Come on!" he yelled. "Let's go! Let's go!"

In a slow, simultaneous lifting of their heads, his fellow crew members looked toward Peter. Each of their bone-white faces now resembled that Messerschmitt fighter pilot, their crazed expressions accentuated by the same diabolical, black, empty caves for eyes. As their heads reared back in demented laughter, Peter heard more screams.

This time, they were coming from him.

***

Awaking with a throat feeling as dry as the Libyan desert but a shirt damp with sweat, Peter tried to shake those nightmarish images away. Passing off the disturbing dream as a case of nerves, he whispered a silent prayer, hoping it didn't foretell an omen—an inescapable concern he needed to immediately banish from his thoughts.

***

"Bail out! Bail out! Bail out!"

The thundering shouts from Pilot Ronald Abernathy reverberated through every headset as the engine destruction caused from their proximity to the refinery explosions left Peter's B-24 incapable of flying any farther. After an inconsequential forty-mile escape, Abernathy frantically surveyed the areas below, looking for an open field. Struggling to hold the plane level for as long as possible, he hoped to give his men enough time to eject.

As the fire from the number three engine roared through the interior, bombardier Alberto Lombardi prayed for himself and his men as he jumped out of the open bomb bay doors. Seeing two other surviving members of his crew floating down in the distance, he cried out in despair as he viewed the plane hurtling toward what appeared to be an agricultural field with trees — too many to allow any chance for a miracle landing. His anguished wails followed as his remaining B-24 brothers crashed into the trees, the bomber exploding into a horrifying mass of flames and surging black smoke.

The plane went down over Sinaia, Prahova County, in Romania's Bucegi Mountains. Of the ten airmen on board, only the three men able to eject survived. Through an edict issued by Queen Helen, the queen mother of Romania, decreeing that all prisoners must be protected and treated with respect, Alberto Lombardi's compassionate captors allowed him and the two others to live — due in no small part by not turning them over to the Germans.

In what could only be seen as a miracle, Peter Levy's burned and broken body was found among a group of trees over a hundred feet from the crash. His was the only one found, leaving Lombardi and his fellow crewmen to conclude that while the others perished instantly in the explosion, Levy's location at the time of impact allowed his body to be thrown clear of the wreck.

With the blessing of their captors, the men buried Airman Peter Levy in a shallow grave marked with a large rock. He was now back home in his birthplace.

As a certain proclamation had foretold.

***

After the war, at a cost of almost two hundred million dollars, the United States Congress authorized the return of as many dead Americans as could be located for those families requesting that undertaking. In June 1949, aided by Airman Alberto Lombardi's knowledge of the burial spot, the body of Airman Peter Levy was exhumed and flown to America to be interred next to his father and sister in Evergreen Cemetery in Boyle Heights, the city where he had lived most of his life. Nearly six years after that fateful burial in Romania, Peter finally rejoined the other members of his family in eternal peace—and where Naomi would join them when her time came.

With equal amounts of pride and tears and clutching a folded American flag in her lap, Naomi listened, between suppressed coughs, to the military honor given her son. A few minutes later, watching Peter's coffin descend on the casket-lowering device into the earth, her sniffling crested into the heartbreaking sobs of a mother's grief.

Surrounded by several friends and associates, Naomi received their embraces and condolences before they departed, leaving only her three close friends from the hospital remaining. Carol, Emily, and Sandra stood back in silence as they watched Naomi approach the edge of the open burial site.

"Give me a few minutes, girls," she said, turning back and offering a smile. "I'll meet you at the car."

"Take all the time you need, honey," Carol replied.

Sweeping back wisps of brown and graying hair from her forehead, Naomi coughed hard, her shoulders slumping and rocking for several moments before the spasm passed. Collecting herself, she threw several more handfuls of dirt on the coffin and whispered to her son through watery eyes.

"I'm so proud of you, Peter," she said, her voice just louder than a whisper. "We won that damn war thanks to courageous men like you. You never knew how truly bad it was for the Jews, but if you can hear me now, there are six million of them thanking you for avenging their deaths and helping to save us." A dark chuckle followed. "I never told you this, but when you were a baby in Bucharest, you were stolen from me. Yes, you heard me right. Stolen. That was the most scared I ever was. Fortunately, it was only about an hour before you were brought back to me by a couple of Romanies, a brother and sister. I'm pretty sure it was the brother who was responsible, but I knew if I called the police, their entire community would have been punished and forced to leave. I told the woman how the Jews knew what it was like to be persecuted just like them. And due to that German psychopath…well, that's over, and he's dead, thank God."

Turning silent, Naomi gathered her final thoughts, convincing herself that Peter had heard her.

"I got your last letter," she said. "Do you know it was postmarked on your birthday? August first, the day you came into this world and the day you left it." Pausing to let the tears fall, she continued, "I reread it just about every day. After what happened to Camille and learning I couldn't have any more children, you were my pride and joy. Your father's, too. It was a good life we had, wasn't it, Peter?" As the tears reached her chin, she added, "A good life, but way too short."

Naomi paused, taking slow breaths to avoid further coughing. As the last of the Levy family, and knowing her lung cancer diagnosis portended a limited time left, she informed her son about one more thing.

"The day after you were stolen, an old Romani woman predicted you'd be taken from me two more times. It frightened me, of course, to hear such disturbing talk, but I never took what she said seriously. Well, it turns out the war took you away from me, so I admit she was half right. But you can't be taken from me anymore, can you, my son? And now it looks like I'll be joining you soon. I've got a space waiting, and when my time comes, I'll die in peace, knowing the four of us will finally be together, forever."

Together, yes. But forever, Naomi? And just the four of you?

Sometimes, the Devil laughs as people plan.

CHAPTER FOUR
TERRENCE COVINGTON

March 2017—five months before the seventy-fourth anniversary of Peter Levy's death

"Hello, everyone. My name is Marjorie Goodwin, and welcome to the Craft and Folk Art Museum's final walking tour of Evergreen Cemetery. I hope you all brought your most comfortable shoes because we'll be covering much of the sixty-seven acres of this Los Angeles landmark."

Turning her head to the left, Marjorie smiled at the dapper, six-foot tall, salt-and-pepper-haired African American man missing a small portion of his left eyebrow. Wearing a turquoise wool beret, a black-and-cream-checkered pullover sweater, a black turtleneck, and gray corduroy pants, he smiled back, waiting for her introduction.

"I can't think of a better person to lead us on our tour today because nobody knows the history of Evergreen Cemetery as well as he does. This handsome man on my left is Mr. Terrence Covington, and he's been a permanent fixture at Evergreen Cemetery since 2004."

"Permanent above ground," Terrence exclaimed.

As Marjorie laughed with the others, she waved him over.

"They're all yours, my friend," she told him. "Take it away."

"Thank you, Marjorie, and welcome to Evergreen Cemetery, everybody, where leaving is a blessing, and staying is depressing."

A combination of laughter and lighthearted remarks from Terrence's ditty followed. Waiting a few moments, he continued.

"As Marjorie told you, my first name is Terrence, but around here, they call me C.T., short for Cemetery Terry." Adjusting his beret and tugging at the bottom of his sweater after a few more chuckles, he said, "Please allow me to give you a brief bio of what brought me to this special place. When my tour of duty ended in Vietnam, I left the military and had a brief career as a boxer. I did OK, winning some, losing some, and holding my own for the most part. But after a particularly memorable knockout punch that I'm reminded of every time I look in the mirror and see a scar where part of my left eyebrow used to be" — lifting the portion of his beret to expose the scar, Terrence pointed to the spot — "I decided it was best to move on."

Readjusting the bill of his beret, he continued his background introduction.

"After my boxing career, I bounced around as a carpenter, a house painter, a cement mason, and spent one forgettable summer as a roofer. So, I got lucky when I finally landed a secure job that I liked here at the cemetery. I think of myself as a utility man, like what a baseball player who plays different positions does. I'm an extra maintenance man for the grounds and a handyman and custodian for the buildings and crematorium. But today, I've been given the chance to get out of my uniform, put on some regular clothes, and talk with you good folks about this amazing place, established in 1867 and containing over three hundred thousand gravesites."

Turning his body to the side and extending his arm, Terrence identified a white structure tall enough to be seen in the distance.

"Before we start our walk, I want you all to look out there. As a vet, I'm honored to bring to your attention that beautiful monument honoring the 442nd Regimental Combat Team. They were known as the Nisei soldiers, second-generation Japanese American volunteers who not only fought for us in World War II but wound up being one of the most decorated units in American history. We'll talk about that later when we visit that section. Evergreen also has other military veterans from as far back as the Civil and Spanish–American Wars to as recently as the war in Iraq. Every Memorial Day, we have a ceremony to honor all the veterans who are buried here."

Turning back again to face the visitors, Terrence waved his hand across the width of the other areas of the cemetery.

"We're also going to visit the gravesites of business leaders who built Los Angeles from the ground up, names just about any Angelino knows, like Isaac Lankershim, Isaac Van Nuys, and John Hollenbeck. For any of you who have gone shopping for groceries at Ralphs market, well, George Ralphs is buried here, too. There are also actors, singers, athletes, and politicians, including former mayors of the city.

We also have a section where the graves of four hundred circus performers and carnival workers from the Pacific Coast Showmen's Association are located. And for any of you who are fans of scary movies, one of our first stops will be the Ivy Chapel, built in the 1890s, where they filmed the funeral scene for Nightmare on Elm Street. So, if you're ready, I am, and off we go."

During the initial part of the walk, Terrence explained that, unlike so many other cemeteries in the country, no ethnicities, "except one," were banned from burials, including, as one might assume, African Americans.

"And this place was established in 1877, so as a Black man, I was happy to learn that," he said. "That's the main reason I purchased a plot here. But unfortunately, like so many neighborhoods, the cemetery was segregated. In addition to those who were white, there are sections for African Americans, Mexicans, Japanese, Armenians, and others. But nowadays it's not divided up except for those who prefer it. My wife is Mexican American, and I'm African American. We wanted our plots to be in a nonsegregated section." Smiling, Terrence added, "So we found a shady spot near a nice Jewish family of four, the Levys."

A woman raised her hand.

"What was the group that wasn't allowed here?" she asked.

"The Chinese people," Terrence answered. "Racism was terrible for them back then. But there is justice in the world, sometimes." Terrence smiled again and paused before continuing. "The owner of Evergreen Cemetery today is Chinese."

After a few laughs and handclaps, Terrence gave a thumbs-up sign.

"Near the end of the tour I'll show you an area near the crematorium that was called Potter's Field. It was the one place where the Chinese could bury their dead as long as they paid. But burial was free for everyone else. Here's a story for you. In 2005, when the Metro Line was being built at First Street, the remains of one hundred seventy-four skeletons were discovered. They also found opium pipes, rice bowls, jade bracelets, and Asian coins, so it left no doubt it was the Chinese portion of Potter's Field that was uncovered."

"What happened to the skeletons?" a man asked.

"A memorial wall to honor them was constructed," Terrence answered. "And all one hundred seventy-four are now buried in the cemetery near that wall."

***

Terrence's sixty-nine-year-old body remained in good enough shape to retain the ability to handle the heavy machinery required for the extra blowing, hedge trimming, and weeding that the regular four-man crew occasionally fell behind on, especially during the warmest months. Evergreen now employed its fourth landscape maintenance company since his hiring and each one seemed no better than the previous crew, still requiring a good amount of his time on the grounds.

A series of overdue rainstorms from January and February brought an abundance of lush green weeds scattered throughout. Despite the extra workload, the gratifying memory of leading yesterday's tour brought a light-footed energy to the man—a picture of purposeful contentment in his khaki-colored pants and forest green, buttoned-down shirt with the Evergreen Cemetery name stitched in yellow above the left pocket.

Terrence stopped and looked toward the sky, pausing to admire two box-shaped clouds drifting along in feathery innocence. He enjoyed this part of his job, working outdoors and moving from one familiar gravesite to the next. Many of them contained photos of the deceased with inscriptions often weatherworn, highlighting particular personal histories. Through the years, he'd developed an imaginary friendship with several names and faces, stopping at times to converse with his favorites.

Terrence held a special place in his heart for Biddy Mason, a woman born into slavery in Georgia in 1818. Mason's freedom came when her owner moved from Utah to California, believing he could maintain his ownership of her. However, with California a free state by law, her slavery ended with the move. Mason died in 1891, but not before amassing great wealth in real estate, becoming the first African American woman to own land in Los Angeles and a beloved and respected philanthropist for the poor. Never learning to read or write, she signed her contracts with a stylish "X." Mason also cofounded the Los Angeles branch of the First AME Church, Terrence's place of worship.

"Hello, Biddy," he said, turning off his machine. "Lovely day today."

Gazing out at the Hollywood Hills, he smiled at the clarity of the Hollywood sign at the top of the Santa Monica mountains, something not always possible.

"I gave a tour yesterday and brought the group here to see your headstone and tell your story." Giggling, he added,

"But if you can hear me now, then you probably already know that."

Leaning down, he turned his head to the side.

"What'd you say, Biddy? How did it go? I tell you, it went fine, real fine."

Straightening up again, Terrence spotted Hummingbird and Dragonfly, two homeless regulars he'd befriended, sitting across the street against a brick wall of a boarded-up antique clothing store on the corner of Evergreen and Caesar Chavez Avenue.

"Hey, guess what, Biddy?" he asked. "I finally finished paying off the gravesites for Juana and me. Yeah, one day, we'll be sleeping next to that Jewish family I told you about. I looked up their burial records and they seemed like good folk. The mother was a nurse, just like you were when you started out. And the son fought and died in World War Two doing something real honorable. Sad, they lost a baby girl at childbirth, and the father died of tuberculosis before the war. But now all four of 'em are together forever, and me and Juana will be their neighbors."

Surveying the large stretch of surrounding weed growth, Terrence took a deep breath, taking his shoulders on an inhale, exhale, up-and-down ride.

"I better go, Biddy," he said. "As always, it was a pleasure talking with you." Kissing his hand, he kneeled and placed it on her grave for several moments before restarting the weed trimmer and resuming work.

CHAPTER FIVE
UNEXPECTED NEWS

Returning the call from Andrew, the director of operations for the cemetery, Terrence leaned on his weed trimmer like a cane as he waited for him to answer.

"Hey, C.T., where've you been?" Andrew asked. "I left you that message ten minutes ago."

"Sorry, had my weed trimmer on and couldn't hear the phone," Terrence replied. "You said you needed to talk to me. What's up?"

"There's something I want to discuss, but not over the phone," he said. "Can you come to the office? I'll be here for the next couple of hours or so."

Terrence didn't give the request much thought, seeing as how he'd often been called to meet with Andrew through the years about building maintenance issues or additional work needed for upcoming events. Strolling into the office about an hour later, Terrence sat in the chair across from Andrew as he waited for a phone conversation to end.

"I heard things went very well yesterday," Andrew

said, placing his cell phone on his desk. "Marjorie Goodwin called and told me you were fantastic. She said she learned about stuff even she didn't know, and she's given tours here."

"That's nice to hear, Andrew. Thanks. I hope I can do it again sometime."

Andrew stared and smiled before sitting up and leaning forward, placing his arms on the desk. Terrence sensed something different than previous conversations with him. The usual amiable yet businesslike attitude from his boss now showed a person appearing to be in some kind of pain or discomfort, with his narrowing eyes and tightening mouth.

"You OK?" Terrence asked.

Andrew took a noticeable breath before answering.

"Terrence, I'll just get right to the point."

Leaning back in surprise at being called by his real first name, a rarity coming from Andrew, Terrence waited in a sudden feeling of suspense.

"The owner is looking for ways to cut back on expenses," he told him. "That not only includes changing vendors we work with but also our in-house payroll." Andrew took another breath, paused, and shook his head. "I'm sorry, Terrence, and I don't agree with it, but he wants to replace you with some fresh-faced kid he can pay less money."

Terrence lowered his head, the top of his new green Evergreen Cemetery cap replacing the astonished facial expression shown moments before.

"The boss is very appreciative of your years here," Andrew said. Clearing his voice, he continued. "And along with what you already have coming, the remainder of this pay period and your accrued vacation pay, he wants to pay you an extra month's salary. If you look for another job, I'll give you the kind of praiseworthy reference you deserve. You've certainly earned that."

Terrence raised his head, his pain exposed in the moist, reddish-white background surrounding those kindhearted brown eyes.

"I don't want another job, Andrew," he said, his voice hushed as if talking to himself. "I like it here, I'm happy here, and it's just not right."

"I'm sorry, Terrence," Andrew said, nodding his head back and forth. "There's nothing more I can do."

Told to return the next day to pick up his check, Terrence glanced at Andrew's administrative assistant, Ramona, before leaving the office. Her reluctance to look at him, unusual for her customarily exuberant self, told him all he needed to know about whether she'd already been informed. Without stopping, he exited the building and took the fifteen-minute walk toward his gravesite for one more look at his future permanent home.

Staring at the two markers, he reflected on his life and whispered a prayer for Juana, now legally blind, with macular degeneration in both eyes. Having been a librarian for much of her adult life, Juana's love of books had evolved into a fervent determination to learn Braille, something still requiring practice after starting a couple of months earlier. Terrence spent enough evenings assisting her that he had learned a few letters himself, writing them with their corresponding dot arrangements on a sheet of paper while testing her.

Terrence approached the grave of Peter Levy, pausing to look again at the man's black-and-white photograph, which he'd examined before. He saw the facial resemblance to Naomi Levy, Peter's mother, whose color photograph appeared on the gravesite next to her son's. Terrence reread the headstone of this World War II airman, a young man not far removed from his teenaged years who possessed an easy smile and a joyful expression, belying the heroic guts required for his job.

Airman Peter Levy
8th Air Force 44th Bomb Group
August 1, 1920–August 1, 1943

"Maybe we'll swap war stories one day, Peter," he murmured.

Walking away, Terrence approached a curved section of the grounds, veering away from where he'd stood a minute before. Turning his head for a final glance back, his eyes skimming past the green, weedy sprouts from the recent rains, he halted in midstride at the sight of something extraordinary, perhaps even unexplainable.

Observing a large crow perching on top of Peter's headstone, he watched it fly off in a rapid, ascending flight above a large eucalyptus tree, circle back, and then dive-bomb, beak first, into the engraved part of the stone. Assuming the crow to be dead after slamming into the marker with a blood-curdling squawk, Terrence's eyes widened in disbelief as the bird regained its footing, shook its body, and repeated the same crazy maneuver. This time, however, the crow remained motionless.

Terrence remained in place, waiting to see if the bird would move again, but if seeing was believing, what he witnessed next made him wonder if he was hallucinating. The air around the dead crow started turning blurry, the way heat rises from a barbeque pit. While continuing to stare at this unexplainable phenomenon, the bird's feathers started peeling away, exposing much of its pale gray skin. A part of him wanted to take a closer look, but the pain of his conversation with Andrew had affected him too much to stick around any longer.

"Time to get out of here," he muttered.

Sitting motionless for a few minutes before starting his car, Terrence stared out from the windshield of his silver Toyota Corolla at a couple of runners working their way along the exposed part of the Evergreen jogging path. He remembered the excitement expressed by many in the Boyle Heights community from the first day of the path's construction to the celebration of its completion in 2008. Now, in his combination of a broken heart and impotent helplessness, that jogging trail represented nothing more than a mile and a half of decomposed granite, continuing in an unending loop along the perimeter of a place he'd grown to love but was now unceremoniously forced to leave.

Driving west from the cemetery on North Evergreen Avenue, Terrence spotted Hummingbird and Dragonfly stationed in the same graffiti strewn location as earlier that day—half a block up from the cemetery on Caesar Chavez Avenue between a tattoo parlor and an abandoned bakery. Observing Hummingbird sweeping the sidewalk with the determination of someone cleaning the floor of their own home, his eyes veered toward Dragonfly wiping their tent with a wet rag. Using water taken in a bucket, presumably from the hose bib adjacent to the old bakery, the man's focus on a small spot seemed no less conscientious than someone washing their shiny new sports car. Feeling sadness over an added sense of loss, knowing he'd never see these colorful, down-on-their-luck people again, two kind souls with whom he'd struck up a friendship, Terrence pulled over to the curb to park his car to say goodbye.

Through the brightness of the spring sunshine, Hummingbird's matching attire of a neon-purple T-shirt, purple pants, and purple gift-wrapping ribbon for her chest-length, light brown pigtails, created a strong contrast against the city-gray sidewalk and her black, high-top sneakers. Possessing a wide, fleshy face enhanced by her petite nose and almost imperceptible neck, every move she made washing that sidewalk seemed as if her entire compact body lacked the ability to have the upper half move in a separate direction from her lower half. How north moved, south followed. Standing about five feet, five inches, her round, chubby physique contrasted with Dragonfly's tall, thin frame, bringing to Terrence's mind a type of Laurel and Hardy likeness, but the other way around.

Dragonfly wore his familiar, wide-brimmed straw gardening hat with dangling frayed edges resembling sand-colored worms. The extended brim created a shadow on the scruffy, long face, and sunken eyes, hiding a discernable scar that Terrence observed from a previous conversation when Dragonfly removed the hat to wipe sweat from his forehead. Etched from the left side of his forehead to the bottom of his ear, the scar manifested an undoubtedly memorable encounter, but Terrence knew better than to ask.

The hole in the right knee of his jeans joined in homeless harmony with the small hole at the front of his left sneaker, exposing the hint of a big toe. His baggy red sweatshirt, reading "Bryce Canyon National Park," appeared to be the same one worn by Hummingbird the last time they talked, when she wore red pants with matching red ribbons on her pigtails. Although the wear and tear of their clothes seemed obvious, Terrence respected the dignity shown in their continual ability to find ways to keep their clothes and themselves clean.

"Hey, how ya doin,' C.T.?" Hummingbird said, offering Terrence an exuberant smile.

Dragonfly turned and pounded his fist against his heart.

"C.T., my man!" he shouted. "We ain't ready for no crematorium yet, amigo, you know what I mean? And I ain't got no pocket change for you neither."

Terrence laughed and reached for his wallet. As he always did in his previous conversations with them, he doled out a few dollars, repeating the same line each time.

"Don't spend it all at the racetrack."

That remark elicited laughter whenever he said it, as if each time was the first time. Terrence enjoyed seeing them laugh, knowing that homelessness was never synonymous with anything joyful.

"Looks like I caught you guys doing some housecleaning," he said. "When you bring your shopping carts in that tent at night, there can't be much room left. You two sleep OK in there?"

"He don't play no mariachi music between my legs,

if that's what you mean, you dirty old man," Hummingbird replied, chuckling and flashing a wink. "I'm a good white girl, and 'Fly's a Latino gentleman. We give each other all we need — companionship and protection."

"I had my share of good times when I was a younger man," Dragonfly said. "But it got me in a lot of trouble, too, you know what I mean?" With a slow, repetitious nod of his head, he added, "I got me a history, brother."

"All I know is, I'd rather be here with 'Fly than where I come from," Hummingbird said. "My parents were drunks, my sister got knocked up and disappeared, and my brother's in jail for killin' somebody. Hey, maybe it was my father he killed, but I ain't sayin' 'cause he was a mean man, and whatever bad thing came his way, he deserved." Shaking her head, Hummingbird narrowed her eyes and looked out into the street. "Yes, sir. He had it comin.'"

"I have something to tell you," Terrence said. "Found out a little while ago that they're laying me off. Today was my last day at the cemetery. Shocked me, man, big-time. Told me they want to save money and hire a young guy."

"Oh, man, I'm sorry, C.T.," Dragonfly said. "All the years you gave that place, damn, that don't seem right. What are you gonna do now?"

"C'mon, 'Fly, give the man a chance to breathe. He just found out today."

"Hummingbird's right," Terrence said. "I don't know what I'll do. I got me a smart wife at home, and maybe she'll help me figure it out. I'm on my way there now, but when I saw the both of you, I just wanted to say goodbye and good luck."

Hummingbird placed the broom handle against the lip of the water bucket before giving Terrence a hug.

"You're a fine man, C.T.," she said. "I'm gonna miss you."

Dragonfly extended his hand to shake.

"Day to day, there ain't no feelin' comfortable out here," he told him. "A lot of bad people, you know what I mean? You're one of the good ones, C.T."

"Thanks, Dragonfly," he replied. "You keep watching out for each other, OK?"

"If somebody ever tries to hurt my 'Fly, they're gonna have to get through me first," Hummingbird said. "And good luck with that."

As Terrence headed toward his car, he stopped, turned around, and walked back.

"I just thought of something," he said. "I never asked where you came up with your names. Do you mind me asking?"

Hummingbird and Dragonfly looked at each other and smiled.

"You ever take the time to watch a hummingbird or a dragonfly, C.T.?" Hummingbird asked.

"Yeah, of course," he answered. "Amazing little things."

"Oh yeah, they're amazing, all right," Hummingbird said. "Nothin' can catch 'em, and nothin' can keep 'em down. No matter what's going on, whenever they want to, they just swoop and zoom and fly away. Anywhere, anytime." She smiled again and took a breath, her face taking on a pensive expression. "We have a dream, a wish, that someday we'll turn into one of them ourselves. He'll be a dragonfly, and I'll be a hummingbird. And when that day comes, we'll fly away from these streets as fast as our little wings can take us."

CHAPTER SIX
ON THE WAY HOME

Entering the I-5 freeway toward his home in South Pasadena, Terrence turned up the volume on Satellite radio's jazz station when Ben Webster's soulful version of 'When I Fall in Love' started playing. The calming saxophone therapy eased his edginess and brought back a beautiful memory from his wedding day. As he listened and hummed along, he reflected on the moment he met Juana on an autumn afternoon in 1999.

A week removed from quitting his roofing job and seeking a way to quiet his frustrations and ascertain his next move, Terrence strolled through Eisenhower Park in the city of Arcadia on a cool, clear Sunday, enjoying the fresh air, green grass, and lush tree scenery. Dressed in a black, long-sleeved Playboy Jazz Festival T-shirt, blue jeans, and a zipped-up gray sweatshirt, he placed the hood of the sweatshirt over his head when he stopped in a cooler, shaded part of the park to watch a white woman in the playground pushing a laughing young boy on a swing. While reminiscing about his own playground days as a kid, he noticed the woman repeatedly turning her head to look at him with what seemed like an expression of concern. Grabbing the child's hand in sudden haste, she yanked him from the swing and hurried away toward the parking lot, to the dismay of the child, now heard bawling in the distance.

Terrence didn't need an explanation for the woman's abrupt departure, facing the hurtful reminder, once again, of the suspicion created by the color of his skin. He stood still, staring at nothing specific but flashing back on experiences with racism that he encountered from his childhood, his teenaged years, and the military.

"I saw that," a voice behind him said. "Looks like that stupid woman couldn't leave fast enough."

Snapping back from his momentary mind drift, Terrence turned and saw a pretty Latina woman who appeared to be in her early-to-mid forties sitting on a bench. Wearing dark blue cotton pants, a caramel-colored knit sweater, a black top, and a leopard-print brown and yellow scarf around her neck, she gripped a book in one hand and a Starbucks coffee cup in the other. Terrence felt drawn to her intense yet caring expression, conveying an alluring combination of compassion and wisdom.

"Life isn't fair, but some of us know that more than others," she said. "I'm in charge of a local library, and you should see the looks I often get when people find out this middle-aged Mexican lady is a professional with a degree in library science."

"I see a Mexican lady, but one who doesn't look middle-aged yet," Terrence replied.

"Well, aren't you the charmer," she said. "I hope you

don't mind me saying what I did about that woman, but I tend to speak my mind when I don't like what I see and damn the consequences."

"A lot of people don't speak up at all," Terrence said. "And that's part of the problem, isn't it? Think you would have said something to that woman if she had walked past you instead?"

"Honestly, I'm not sure," she answered, "but that's only because she had the child with her. Why expose him to the real world of adults when he's so young? He'll have plenty of time to learn our ways and get dirty like the rest of us."

The woman grabbed her handbag from the bench and placed it on the other side of her. Scooting over, she said, "My name's Juana. Care to sit down?"

That beginning moment turned into a conversation lasting for the remainder of the afternoon. The next day, Terrence met Juana for lunch during her break and learned about her brief marriage to a man in San Diego, which ended after she arrived home early from work to find him in bed with her sister. Once the divorce was finalized, she moved to Los Angeles for an assistant librarian job offer, eventually working her way up to her current head librarian job. Juana never remarried and remained childless, living with periodic regrets over both decisions but satisfied with her life's path.

Terrence told Juana about his intention to marry his high school sweetheart until postponing it due to the draft and eventually being shipped off to Vietnam. As with several of his brothers from the war facing the same circumstance, his girl back home moved on. That wound healed, but upon returning to civilian life, his coping mechanisms for dealing with society in general didn't fare well. It took some effort and some mental health aid from the Veteran's Administration, but in time, he regained his sense of self. He told Juana he never married and, like her, remained childless.

"I won't speak for the other vets, but for me, it was that war, the things I saw, that made it hard to keep things real with a woman, let alone start a family," he told her.

The relationship between the two of them grew into a love affair. Juana encouraged him to take the job at Evergreen Cemetery, and soon after his hiring, they got married — a small affair in the First AME Church. For their first dance, to the piano accompaniment of a church member, Juana's friend sang "When I Fall in Love," a favorite of theirs.

***

The fiery words of loud racist taunts flew like bullets toward the elderly Asian woman standing in front of a bakery shop across the street from the supermarket where Terrence stopped for groceries. Standing by his open trunk, he observed several people keeping their distance and staring, but nobody helping, including a man and a woman filming the incident with their phones.

"Jesus!" he cried out.

Dashing toward the abusive man, Terrence arrived too late to prevent the woman from being knocked to the ground and kicked.

"Get the hell away from her!" he yelled, shoving him hard in the chest.

Stumbling back several steps, the bald, heavyset, bearded man shouted an expletive and racist slur at Terrence before stepping forward and taking a wild swing at his head. Dodging his fist with the defensive skill of a former boxer, Terrence countered with a solid, bone-crunching punch to the middle of the man's nose, driving him back in shouts of pain and forcing him to flee.

"Nai Nai!" a woman screamed.

Wheeling around, Terrence saw a young Asian woman cradling the fallen woman as she remained on the ground. Ignoring the stares and inquiries about her condition from the suddenly concerned people standing around, Terrence kneeled alongside the two of them, inspecting the elderly woman's tearful, frightened face. No cuts or bruises were visible, and after a couple of minutes observing the woman's mental state, as her head lay cradled in the young woman's lap, Terrence believed she seemed well enough for him to offer a suggestion for the next thing to do.

"I think she'll feel better if she's off this dirty sidewalk and back on her feet," he told her.

Looking at him through watery eyes, the young woman nodded and, in another minute, stood with her arm wrapped around the old woman's shoulder, speaking to her in another language.

"She thinks she's OK," she said to Terrence, wiping away her tears. "Thank you, thank you so much for protecting my grandmother. And she wants me to tell you she's very grateful for what you did."

Terrence studied the wrinkled face of the elderly woman before speaking to the younger one, a petite, short-haired, college-aged woman with glasses, dressed in jeans and a gray Cal State LA sweatshirt.

"Physically, your grandmother looks fine for now," he said. "But you should keep a close eye on her over the next few days to make sure nothing is wrong. Sometimes, injuries don't show up right away. And with the big scare she just had, it's her mental state you want to keep track of, too. I have a feeling this whole ugly thing will sink in later."

"Yes, yes, of course," she said. "What's your name, sir?"

"Terrence," he answered. "And yours?"

"Tiffany."

"You called your grandmother, Nai Nai. Is that what it means?"

Tiffany nodded. "It's a Chinese term," she said. "I've called her that name my whole life." Lowering her gaze, Tiffany looked at the yellow lettering above the pocket of his dark green shirt. "Is that where you work? Evergreen Cemetery?"

Terrence hesitated before deciding not to dwell on the details of the truth. This wasn't the time or place for an explanation—especially one that didn't concern this woman.

"Yes," he answered. "Evergreen Cemetery."

CHAPTER SEVEN
JUANA COVINGTON

Sitting up with her knees on the carpet, Juana held two black Chinese checker marbles in her left hand and one in the right, waiting to hear Nigel's voice from the other side of the twenty-foot-long carpeted room of her apartment.

"OK, I'm standing behind three of the marbles," he told her. "A green one, a red one, and a blue one, all in a row about a foot apart from each other. You hit two on Wednesday, so maybe you can do it again, Juana."

She smiled. "Just continue counting to ten nice and slow for each throw," she said.

As Nigel started counting, Juana focused on his voice for several more seconds before rolling her first marble toward the target area.

"Oh, almost," he said. "It was getting there but stopped a little short, but only about maybe six inches away. Roll the next one a little harder. Should I start counting again?"

"It's my only chance, honey," she replied. "I can't see anymore, so your voice helps me understand the distance and direction."

Nigel started counting again.

As he reached number six, Juana experienced a clear, flashing image of her black marble grazing the blue one. While she could no longer see with her eyes, she saw clearly in her mind. Hesitating several moments to allow this recently recurring and unsettling phenomenon to register, she rolled her second marble.

"Oh, oh, yes, yes, yes, all right!" Nigel cried. "You did it, Juana. You hit one."

Listening to the excitement in Nigel's voice right before contact, Juana realized that her brief mental picture of the two marbles connecting conveyed a reality rather than a mere possibility. Hearing the 'click' of her marble colliding with the other brought a disturbing sensation rather than a happy one.

"Which marble did I hit?" she asked.

"The blue one," he answered.

Juana lowered her head, her concern growing over the sudden reawakening of these premonitions that started several weeks ago after thirty-seven years of inactivity. That unexplainable phase of her life seemed a lifetime ago — something she assumed to be a closed chapter from those periodic episodes starting in her late teens and continuing until her mid-twenties. She remembered the first one, of course, occurring while standing onstage during her high school graduation when she was eighteen years old.

***

"This is taking forever, Maggie," Juana whispered, standing erect in her cap and gown next to her friend who, coincidentally, shared her last name.

"That's what we get for having a last name that starts with an 'A,' and they go in alphabetical order," Maggie replied, snickering. "There's only a few more names to go, so hang in there, girl."

"Look at Jimmy Reyes," Juana said, a childish breathiness to her voice. "He looks so cute in his cap and gown."

"You've had a crush on him for as long as I've known you," Maggie replied.

"Yeah, I know," Juana said, a smile of resignation on her face. In a sudden loss of the moment, as if a fast-forward button was briefly pressed, Juana visualized Jimmy tripping on the steps approaching the stage, causing the girl ahead of him, Gloria Rasmussen, to fall to her knees. As if vanishing like a ripple in a pond, Juana's view of the present reappeared just in time to see Jimmy trip on the stairs, bringing Gloria down with him—an exact replication of the scene playing in her mind moments before.

"Oh my God!" Maggie blurted out, her giggling joining that of many of their classmates. Juana remained silent, her blank, solemn expression conveying a different mood than the others. Turning toward her friend, Maggie gave Juana a playful nudge.

"Don't worry, Juana, he's OK. I think you're the only one who didn't laugh."

"Something really weird just happened," Juana told her.

"What?" Maggie asked.

"I...I don't know," she replied. "I mean, I saw

something, but…but I don't…"

Juana shook her head back and forth several times as if trying to shake a fly off her face.

"Just forget it," she said. "Whatever it was, it's gone now."

"Maybe later you can ask Jimmy if he'll let you rub it where it hurts," Maggie whispered.

"Shut up, girl," Juana said, giving her friend a playful poke with her elbow.

The following years produced occasional intuitions in different places under various circumstances, but due to their harmless and inconsequential scenarios, Juana accepted them as nothing more than an innocently weird brain activity she developed somehow, even going so far as to consider them cool things to be proud of as if she were a comic book character with secret powers. However, a couple of years after marrying her college sweetheart, on a day when she left work early with a worsening cold, the jolting image of her husband making love to her sister hit Juana like a gut punch as she returned home and pulled into her parking spot.

Hurrying from the car to her apartment, Juana worked the key into the lock, fumbling a bit at first with trembling hands. Offering no second chance opportunity for reconciliation with her husband—or her sister— a divorce eventually led Juana to Los Angeles with the acceptance of her application for an assistant librarian job. In moments of reflection, Juana felt grateful for what her strange ability exposed that day despite the heartbreak.

Several weeks later, however, on a rainy winter night, as she pulled back the sheets to go to bed, any gratitude she felt about her periodic ability to see things before they happened turned into a desperate desire to make them stop. From out of nowhere, a sudden repulsive image of a bald, scary-looking man with beady, bloodshot eyes and a demonic laugh appeared like a monster in her mind, eliciting a muted scream and a drive to bury her head under the pillow. Juana prayed that sleepless night and for many nights afterward. Despite nothing coming to fruition after that frightening image vanished, she asked God to make this ability cease for good — one she'd never wanted anyway.

For the next thirty-seven years, her prayers seemed answered. Now, for a reason she didn't understand, the premonitions had returned.

***

The incident with the marbles now marked the fourth recent instance of seeing momentary visuals of an impending event inside her head. The first of those four fooled her into thinking what she saw originated from a dream. Her sight dwindling down to its current level of seeing nothing but shadows, Juana figured she must have dozed off after experiencing a vision of Terrence opening the door and holding a bouquet of pink roses — her favorite flower and color.

When he arrived home with a dozen pink roses from the market, Juana reacted in stunned silence, snapping out of it only when he asked if she felt all right. Startled by the possible revival of a long-dormant part of her life, one she never wanted to encounter again, she offered a sincere yet insecure smile for her husband, hugging him with a combination of outward love and secretive fear.

A week later, as Juana sat in her chair listening to a

Diana Krall CD, an overhanging branch from the neighbor's sycamore tree snapped and fell on a parked car, setting off a lengthy car alarm. Juana saw and heard it coming minutes before. This second experience, within a short time, convinced her that the capacity for having premonitions not only still existed within her but had activated again, rattling her usual stoic nature. Despite this unsettling discovery, she refused to confess anything about those days to Terrence, determined to keep that part of her life in a time capsule drifting further away into space.

Two nights ago, however, after the fleeting image of Terrence cutting himself while chopping an onion preceded a yelp and several expletives from the kitchen, that unnerving feeling gripped her with dread, afraid of what might come next.

And today, even with an innocent game of marbles, the return of something unexplainable and uncontrollable, maybe potentially fearful, drove Juana to reconsider her resolve not to tell Terrence.

"Juana, are you OK?" Nigel asked. "You did it. You hit the marble. Aren't you happy?"

"I'm sorry, Nigel," she said, a rapid shake of her head bringing her back to the present. "I was just thinking of something." Holding the final marble in her closed fist, she shook it like a gambler preparing to toss a pair of dice. "Let's see if I can do it again."

"One, two, three, four, five..."

After Juana rolled her last marble, Nigel announced the misguided throw like a baseball announcer.

"Here it comes, ladies and gentlemen, the marble's

getting closer, closer, and...oh, not this time, too far to the left. But let's hear it for Juana Covington, everybody. Another marble hit!"

"Thank you, my friend," she said. "Now, please help this old lady up and into the kitchen. I've got some chocolate chip cookies and milk for the winner before he starts his homework."

Gripping a white cane in her left hand, Juana waited for Nigel to hook his arm around her right one before moving toward the kitchen. At sixty-two years old and standing five feet, seven inches tall, Juana retained a slim figure and the mostly wrinkle-free face of a younger woman. The steady erosion of her sight, however, left her struggling in a murky world of muddy gray and feeling older than her age. Her large, dark brown eyes, at one time a noticeable feature on her pretty face, now stared with an indirect and vacant gaze into the dark blur of life around her.

Juana had started playing marbles with Nigel from the days when her eyesight and high index prescription lenses allowed her to still compete and connect on occasion with the awaiting targets. On Wednesdays and Fridays, after the school bus dropped him off, he'd stay with her for a couple of hours while his hairstylist mother, Krissy, finished work. Every other week, Krissy came to Juana's apartment to wash and maintain her fashionably short white hair, which she parted on the right and brushed across with a partial covering of her upper forehead. Juana's bushy eyebrows, although flecked with gray, still retained most of her original black hair color, and when she smiled, the soft, light brown skin of her cheeks exposed dimples from the corners of her mouth to the bottom of her wide nose.

A rapping of knuckles on the door signaled Krissy's arrival. Pushing his science book aside, Nigel rose from the table to open the door for his mother. Tussling her son's bushy, reddish-brown hair as she entered, Krissy made Nigel giggle, exposing the gap in his mouth. At eleven years old, Nigel's frail, four-foot, two-inch stature invited occasional teasing from certain boys at school. A shy kid who didn't easily make friends, he retained a self-confidence instilled in him by his mother, having overcome her own days of teasing as a small girl with freckles and frizzy hair.

"How was your marble game today?" Krissy asked.

"I must be a glutton for punishment," Juana said, remaining in her chair. "I keep trying, but it's not like it used to be."

"You're getting better, Juana," Nigel said. "You hit another one today and came close on some others."

"Gather up your stuff," Krissy said. "Thanks, Juana. Are we still on for Monday?"

"Getting my hair done is one of the few pleasures left for this old, blind lady," she answered. "I look forward to it."

When the door closed, Juana remained in her beige leather chair, contemplating what occurred during the game.

"Why is this happening to me again?" she whispered. "Should I tell Terrence? He already worries so much about me. And now this?" Closing her eyes, Juana took a slow, extended breath, accepting a reality but feeling unprepared.

"I'm going to tell him," she said, speaking louder this time. "I'm too old for this. Too damn blind for it. They've come back, and I'm scared."

***

Terrence's news about his layoff sabotaged Juana's decision to divulge her secret over dinner. Suppressing her own apprehension, she focused on comforting her husband, offering support for whatever came next.

"I've got my Roth and 401k accounts, and I suppose I can start collecting Social Security," he said, shaping the meatballs on the counter as Juana sat at the kitchen table. "I think we'll be OK. At least, I hope so."

"It's just not right, Terrence. You worked at Evergreen for seventeen years, and this is what they do to you?"

"Tell you what, Juana," he said. "Let's not talk about this anymore tonight. I got a bottle of Chianti at the market, and I'm ready for a large glass. Care to join me?"

"Absolutely," she replied.

After a gentle clinking of glasses and the initial sips, Terrence reached out and grasped Juana's hand.

"I love you, lady," he said.

"I love you more," she replied.

"You always say that."

Juana chuckled. "Just speaking from the heart, baby."

"How was your day today?" he asked.

Juana offered a tired smile, feeling the bothersome fatigue she'd recently started struggling with.

"Well, on a good note, I learned some more letters on my alphabet flash cards," she said. "I only have six more to go until I reach 'Z.'"

"Wow," Terrence said, caressing her hand. "You're almost there, Juana. When you think you're ready for that computer connector we talked about, just say the word."

"That day can't come soon enough," she said. "Internet, here I come. Those cards I'm learning from are so clever, with a raised outline of an object in the center that starts with the letter of the card. They have the Braille dots above it and a raised outline of that specific letter below it. Today, I learned 'P,' 'Q,' 'R,' and 'S.' Puzzle, Quail, Rocket, and Spoon."

Terrence nodded his head in admiration.

"Do you mind showing me after dinner?" he asked. "I could use the distraction. Watching you work with those things is amazing to me."

Juana smiled. "Depends on how much wine I have tonight," she said. "Drink too much, think too little."

"I'm pretty sure I remember the first four letters," he said. "'A' had a black dot in the upper left corner, 'B' had a second black dot right below the one for 'A.' 'C' maybe had two black dots on the right side, one on top and one below it, and 'D' had four black dots, right? I think they were two across the top and two... yeah, two below those." Terrence reached for his wine. "How'd I do?"

"You got the 'A' and 'B' right," she said, chuckling, "but go sit in the corner because you messed up the other two."

Taking a large sip, Terrence held his wineglass in the air for a few additional seconds and stared at the tender, discolored flesh on his right knuckle.

"Oh, yeah," he said, placing the glass back on the table. "I've got something else to tell you."

"Uh-oh," Juana said, grimacing. "Do I want to hear this?"

"You know that bakery shop across from the market?"

Juana's recurring premonitions remained unmentioned for the rest of the evening.

CHAPTER EIGHT
CROWS

With rain in the nighttime forecast and the swelling of darkening clouds as confirmation, Terrence drove into the cemetery to park his car and collect his final check. Feeling sucker punched, the hard-hitting news of his unforeseen termination still felt raw and hurtful as he entered Andrew's office, dragging his feet without much of a desire to converse with the man. Feeling resentful over the cheery expression shown by his now ex-boss, smiling and acting as if nothing had changed, Terrence felt the emotional dagger pushed in even further.

"Sit down, C.T.," Andrew said, gesturing with his hand toward the seat.

Terrence pulled back the chair, positioning himself on the front edge of the cushion in anticipation of a quick chat, check collection, and getaway.

"I thought about calling you on your cell phone," Andrew told him, "but knowing you were coming here today, I much preferred to speak with you in person." Leaning forward, he placed his elbows on the desk and clasped his hands. "I got a call about you this morning and found it so interesting that I called David to tell him about it."

"David?" Terrence said. "As in David, the owner who fired me?"

"Yep," Andrew replied, maintaining his lighthearted demeanor. "And I didn't care that he's on vacation. This was too important."

Terrence leaned back, gripping the arms of the chair.

"A call about me from who?"

"Her name is Tiffany Lin," Andrew said. Pausing for a moment, he asked, "Do you know who that is?"

Terrence looked toward the floor, narrowing his eyes and pondering the name for several moments before the sudden memory of the incident from the day before. The young woman had said her name was Tiffany. He'd told her his name. She'd seen his shirt uniform and left her thinking he still worked at Evergreen.

Terrence nodded. "I met her yesterday," he replied.

Andrew stared in silence for a moment. "And you met her grandmother, too, right?"

Realizing that Tiffany had told Andrew what he'd done to protect the old woman, Terrence described what happened, starting from the moment he heard the racist jerk yelling his hate-filled, anti-Asian slurs and comments.

"I saw people standing around not doing a thing to help," he explained. "A couple of them had their damn phones out filming it, if you can believe that. I couldn't just stand there and do nothing. I had to do something to help that poor woman."

"You're a humble man, C.T.," Andrew said, "so I'll say what Tiffany thinks, what her grandmother thinks, and I do, too. What you did is nothing short of heroic, no matter which way you slice it. Too many people would be afraid to intervene. And the ones taking out their phones to film an old Asian lady being beaten up probably think they're being Good Samaritans just by sending it to the evening news."

Sitting back, Andrew stared at Terrence, a serious expression replacing his smile.

"There's close to a half million Chinese people living in LA County, but in some ways, we're still a small community. Unfortunately, one of those ways is the racism many of us face. Obviously, I don't have to tell you or any Black person about racism, but it wasn't a Black grandmother who got attacked yesterday. It was one of us."

Andrew took a long breath. "David and I are very grateful to you, C.T., and he not only wants me to offer you your job back but with an eight percent raise in pay as well. He also guarantees that you'll have job security as long as he's the owner."

Terrence closed his eyes and lowered his head, his gratitude matched by his disbelief over this twist of fate.

"Is it a deal, C.T.?" Andrew asked. "Will we see you tomorrow?"

For the first time in the last twenty-four hours, Terrence felt the easing of the tension from his neck and shoulders. Rising to his feet, he smiled and extended his hand.

"See you tomorrow, Andrew. I'm very grateful to the both of you, and I know I'll sleep a lot better tonight."

On the way back to his car, Terrence looked ahead and

saw Francisco, the supervisor of the landscape crew, ankle-deep in mud while repairing a broken pipe.

"Hola, Francisco," he said, approaching him from behind.

"Hola, C.T.," Francisco replied, not looking up.

Walking a few more steps until he faced him from the front, Terrence stood in silence as Francisco finished applying glue to a fitting before connecting the two irrigation parts. Looking up from the repair, Francisco's eyes widened.

"¿Qué pasa?" he asked, expressing surprise that Terrence wasn't wearing his Evergreen shirt. "You're not working today?"

"Had some personal stuff to do," Terrence said. "I'll be back tomorrow."

"I got personal stuff to do, too," Francisco said, "but my girlfriend isn't home."

Terrence laughed and started walking away.

"Hey, C.T.," Francisco called out.

Terrence turned around. "Yeah?"

"Your gravesite; remember when you showed me where it was?"

"I remember," he replied. "Why, what about it?"

"You know I always get here before the other guys, right?"

"Yeah, I know," he said. "You and the sun always show up together."

Francisco smiled, nodding his head.

"When I got here yesterday, first thing I did was start trimming the bushes near your spot," he told him. "And I saw something I don't understand. Some dead birds looking really bad, like they were all burned up from a barbeque or something. He shook his head as if trying to release the image from his mind. "Crazy, right?"

Terrence stood in silence, recalling the strange thing he saw the day before and the similar thought of flames from a barbeque.

"There's a family buried on the left side of where my wife and I will be," he said. "Three gravestones. Is that where you saw the birds? In front of those gravestones?"

Francisco nodded. "Sí, how'd you know that?"

"Were they crows?"

"Crows, yeah, so you seen 'em, too?"

"Are they still there?" Terrence asked, ignoring the question.

"No, amigo," Francisco said. "I cleaned it up fast. Didn't want any people seeing that. Might scare 'em, you know?"

"Gracias, Francisco," Terrence said. "Well, whatever it was, I guess that's the end of it. See you tomorrow."

For the remainder of March, all of April, and most of May, no more dead crows appeared, and the thought of that strange event faded from Terrence's mind like the morning after a nighttime dream. In the last week of May, however, unbeknownst to Terrence, a flock of five crows flew down and settled on the ground near the Levy graves. Three of them took off after a brief time, but the remaining two hopped toward Peter's headstone, their repetitious squawks shattering the cemetery silence for anyone within earshot. When they arrived at the middle of his grave, their squawking turned freakish and unearthly, increasing in volume to a maddening pitch. Their claws stopped moving, their bodies started swaying, and their eyes rolled up into their sockets. Several moments later, both birds collapsed, followed by a blurry, bluish wave enveloping the area around their bodies. After another minute, a light gray smoke turned darker until nearly black, and the crows burst into flames.

Like coals from a barbeque.

CHAPTER NINE
UNANSWERED KNOCK

June 15th, 2017—less than seven weeks before the seventy-fourth anniversary of Peter Levy's death

Having now learned the entire Braille alphabet and numbers zero through nine, Juana felt ready to start reading books again. With the Amazon delivery arriving several minutes before, she retrieved the package and shuffled toward her comfortable cushioned chair. Clutching the armrest, she eased down, sat back, opened the parcel, and removed the book. As her first selection, electing to start with a child's book to "baby step" her way into this new challenge, she'd ordered the Braille edition of the first in a series of Little House on the Prairie chapter books—a childhood favorite of hers.

Juana started spider-walking her fingers over the front, back, and side before cradling it in both hands like a prized vase. Following that, she opened the flap, sniffing and stroking the index-card thickness of the pages from the distance of her nose, reveling in the rediscovered, aromatic intoxication of a new book. The pure joy of reacquainting herself with a major part of her life stolen from her brought Juana to tears.

Despite the tragedy of her blindness, the numerous hours dedicated to learning Braille should have been a rewarding time. But the return of the premonitions, now appearing with more frequency, haunted her. Seeing the real-life actuality of the foretold image of Terrence bringing her roses or one rolled marble striking another might be treated as an innocuous and acceptable scenario, but the recent ones, all occurring over the last week, showed different and particularly grim events. Unable to shake off the disturbing scenes, her ability to sleep and move forward with the day suffered as a consequence.

On the previous Sunday, while showering before church, Juana envisioned a car hitting a kid as he rode his bicycle a block up the street. Not knowing the child or the time of the incident, Juana felt powerless to prevent it. Two days later, with Terrence at work, she sat in helplessness as the image of a man assaulting a woman in the driveway next door occurred moments before she heard the woman's scream from outside her window. The worst of all of them happened the day before, as the vision of a man killing himself with a gun inside his car at the corner 7-Eleven revealed itself to her in a sudden image as clear as if she were still blessed with twenty-twenty vision. Her nerves already frayed, the movie-in-her-mind event left her in tears. The soft crying repeated itself while hearing the report of the suicide with Terrence that night on the evening news.

"It's a sad story, Juana, but you didn't know the guy. I'm surprised you're crying over it."

"Terrence," she said, wiping her eyes between sniffles,

"turn off the television. There's something I need to tell you."

Terrence squinted in curiosity before reaching for the remote.

"OK," he said. "The TV's off. Does this have anything to do with why you're crying about the man who killed himself?" he asked.

"Partly," she answered. "But there's a lot more to it than that." Juana paused to take a deep, calming breath, aware of the probability that by the time she finished her confession, Terrence might never think of her the same way.

"You're probably going to have a lot of questions," she said, "but let me finish telling you everything first, all right?"

Terrence settled back in his chair, his full attention on his wife.

"OK, Juana," he replied, "I'm listening."

"I'll start at the beginning," she told him. "Way back to the day of my high school graduation…"

Juana explained everything as Terrance sat motionless and mesmerized. When she finished, and her tears resumed falling, Terrence rose from his chair to kneel and hug his wife. Her soft heaves increased to sobs while he continued keeping his arms wrapped around her head, now pressed against his chest.

"I'm so sorry, Terrence," she murmured. "I've never told anyone about this. Not my parents, my sister, nobody. I didn't want anyone to look at me like I was different, maybe get scared about it, you know?"

Juana pulled back, looking at her husband through blind, watery eyes. "I'm the same person, Terrence. Really, I am. You know that, don't you?"

Terrence cupped his hands on Juana's wet cheeks, holding them there as he brought his face nose to nose with hers.

"I love you more than ever, Juana," he told her. "I'm so glad you finally got this off your chest. How you kept it inside all these years is hard to believe. Now you've got someone to share this with, and no matter what happens, no matter what you see in your head, I'll always be here for you."

Extending her arms, Juana placed them around Terrence's neck and kissed him in a loving and grateful way.

"How 'bout a drink?" he asked.

Terrence strolled to the bar and poured a couple of glasses of wine. Handing Juana her glass, he returned to his chair.

"You say these premonitions started again when I brought you those roses?"

"Yes," she said, "after all those years of nothing, that was the first one. I figured they were a long-ago part of my life that was over with. I never thought about them anymore."

Juana brought the glass to her lips, holding it there in thought before gulping two sips in quick succession. Closing her eyes, she continued, "That man who killed himself today really got to me. It was like I was there with him, and I can't get the image out of my head," she said, both hands clutching her glass. "That haunted look on his face right before the gun went off, and then seeing blood spray on the windows. That's when it ended. Abruptly." Juana snapped her fingers. "Just like that."

"I can't imagine how horrible that must have been for you," Terrence said. "To have to see that."

Nibbling her upper lip, Juana remained silent.

"Would you ever consider talking to a doctor?" Terrence asked. "Maybe even having a CAT scan? There could be an answer there."

Shaking her head, Juana waved that suggestion away.

"No, no doctor," she told him. "Not yet. Let me see where this goes. Maybe these things are like those fireworks shows that save the multiple explosions for the end. Maybe what's going on now will be the last blowout before the smoke clears and the peaceful times resume."

Terrence returned to his kneeling position with his wineglass next to Juana's chair. Clinking his glass with hers, he said, "Here's to getting through the end of the fireworks show. I love you."

"I love you more."

***

In a replay of yesterday, Juana sat on her chair in the early afternoon reading more of Little House on the Prairie. With Nigel's expected arrival in a couple of hours, she first wanted to delve further into the book. Even a children's book offered quite a challenge for a Braille reader in her early stages, and after another fitful sleep, Juana's eyes grew heavy. Placing the book on her lap, she allowed herself to drift off.

And as Juana would soon discover, it doesn't have to be nighttime for a nightmare.

***

Juana's eyesight returned, and she could see everything in real-time. Shivering from a sudden chill now enveloping her, the darkness pervading her unknown location somehow still allowed for a visible outline of moving shadows tilting back and forth like a ship on a stormy sea. Feeling anxious, she grimaced as an unnerving sound echoed in her ears, resembling a combination of a growl and a laugh. Peering deeper into those faint shadows, an image started coming into focus as the sound morphed into a shriek. Juana covered her ears until the unendurable, high-pitched sound abruptly halted. In that sudden silence, as if through the lifting of a semitransparent veil, the full clarity of a towering figure appeared before her.

Juana's immediate recognition of the bald, frightening-looking individual with bloodshot eyes and a snarling expression forced her to turn away in fear. Terrified by her confinement and facing an inability to escape from this unknown blackness, she shut her eyes and covered her face with her hands, panicky over what awaited her. Was he a man? Was he even human? As this thing moved toward her, the surrounding air turned stale and increasingly fetid. Continuing to keep her eyes shut, she realized the unpleasant smell originated from the man's heavy breathing, now close enough to feel on her face.

Contending with an initial inability to speak, Juana finally cried out in fear. "Go away!" she screamed. "Leave me alone!"

The figure remained silent as the increasing intensity of its noxious breathing caused Juana's heart to race faster and her breath to grow short. With nowhere to escape, she threw her arms over her head and screamed again.

***

Holding his white pouch of Chinese checkers marbles, Nigel knocked on Juana's door. Preparing to wait because of the extra time she required nowadays, he felt lighthearted and ready to have fun, like any kid starting summer vacation. Nigel felt extra eager for Juana to open the door so he could teach her a new game, this one requiring the shooter to roll the marble toward the wall from the other side of the room without making contact. The one who comes closest to the wall wins.

Looking at his watch and realizing three minutes had already passed, Nigel rapped his knuckles on the door again, this time with more force and additional knocks. Still no answer.

"Juana?" he said. "Juana, are you there? It's me, Nigel."

Three knocks and another minute later, Nigel shouted this time. "Juana, are you there?"

Disappointed, Nigel returned to his empty apartment and called his mom.

"Juana's not home," he told her. "I'll just watch some TV."

"Really? She's not home?" Krissy replied. "I'm surprised because she told you on Wednesday that she'd see you Friday."

"I kept knocking and even called her name a few times," he explained.

"Nigel, stay on the phone, I need my assistant to do something."

**

Standing next to a client with her hair in curlers, Krissy paused as a sudden worrisome thought struck her. Turning back to the woman, she brushed her hand as she held the cell phone in the air. "I'm sorry, Anita," she said, "I need to finish this phone call with my son. I'll get Theresa to take the curlers out."

With her client taken care of, Krissy walked to a quiet corner and sat in an unoccupied chair.

"I'll try her cell, Nigel. She always keeps it close to her, right? I'll call you right back."

Reaching Juana's voice mail, Krissy left a message before calling Nigel.

"No answer," she told him. "Maybe Terrence took her somewhere, or she just fell asleep. Or maybe she's in the bathroom. Let's hope there's no reason to worry, but I want you to go back right now and try her again. Either way, if she answers or doesn't, hurry and call me back."

A few minutes later, Krissy answered her phone on the first ring.

"She didn't answer!" Nigel shouted. And I pounded on her door real hard, too, like three or four times. I'm scared, Mom. What should we do?"

Krissy tightened her grip on the phone.

"I need to call Terrence," she said. "I have his cell number. If she's not with him, he needs to know immediately that she's not answering the door."

Closing her eyes and focusing on each unanswered ring, Krissy's nervousness increased. Feeling a desperation to reach him and not his voice mail, her heartbeat experienced a sudden acceleration when he answered.

"Hello?"

"Hi, Terrence, it's Krissy Patterson, Nigel's mom."

"Oh, yes, Krissy," he said. "How are you?"

"Sorry to call you at work, but Nigel told me Juana

didn't answer the door, and they always play marbles on Friday. Is she with you?"

Krissy's question received an extended answer of silence before she received the reply she feared.

"No," he said. "Juana should be there."

"I called her a few minutes ago thinking she may be sleeping but got her voice mail. I hope everything's all right."

"Thanks for calling me about this, Krissy," he said. "I've got to get home."

***

After making an immediate phone call to Juana after hanging up, and three more on the way home from his car, Terrence realized he couldn't wait any longer. Calling 9-1-1 and speaking to the dispatcher, he explained the situation and said he'd be there in five minutes. Arriving first, Terrence unlocked the door and rushed toward his wife, slumped motionless in her reading chair. With her book angled in a haphazard direction on the floor, Juana sat with slouching shoulders and her head drooping to the side. Terrence had learned from his days in the military how to check for a pulse in the wrist or neck, and with his fingers placed in one area and then the other, he didn't feel anything. When the paramedics arrived a few minutes later, they found Terrence kneeling on the floor, weeping beside his wife. A brief time afterward, the crew confirmed what he already knew.

Juana was dead.

CHAPTER TEN
MARBLES

July 8, 2017—What would have been Juana's sixty-third birthday and three weeks before the seventy-fourth anniversary of Peter Levy's death

Terrence returned home from his ten-minute walk to the florist. After a bathroom stop, he retrieved his keys for the drive to the cemetery. Approaching his door to leave, he stared at the table still holding Juana's alphabet cards, some in small piles and others scattered.

"Time to put those back in their box, Terrence," he said to himself.

Shaking his head with his eyes still fixed on the cards, he held the bouquet of pink roses in one hand and removed a handkerchief from his pocket.

"The doctor said your heart just gave out," he whispered, wiping his eyes. "And that you died peacefully. Thank God for that." A smile worked its way to his face. "You died doing what you love, Juana. Reading a book."

Terrence locked his door and started walking toward

the garage when he heard a young boy's voice.

"Mr. Covington?"

Turning around, he saw Krissy's son, Nigel, holding a white cloth pouch.

"Hello, Nigel," he said.

"Hi, Mr. Covington," he replied.

Nigel's eyes darted in different directions but not toward Terrence. Biting his upper lip and rubbing small finger circles around his thumb, the boy's nervousness appeared obvious to Terrence.

"What can I do for you, Nigel?"

"I saw you from my window," he said, "walking with those roses. Is it OK to ask if those are for Juana? Are you going to the cemetery to give them to her?"

Terrence smiled. "It's OK to ask me," he said. "Yes, they're for Juana. Today's her birthday, and these are her favorite flowers."

Nigel's eyes widened. "Her birthday? Really?" Grasping his pouch, he stared at it before looking at Terrence. "I talked to my mom about this, and she told me I should ask you if it's OK."

"If what's OK?"

Nigel took a deep breath, his frail shoulders on a slow rise like helium balloons.

"Would you give these marbles to Juana, please?" he asked. "I know she really liked playing, and I want her to have them. Maybe you can put the pouch next to those flowers."

Terrence stared at the boy in silence before reaching into his pocket again for the handkerchief.

"That's a very nice gesture, Nigel," he said, dabbing

away tears. "Your mother knows about this?"

"Yeah, she knows," he answered. "I told her I've been thinking about it ever since the funeral. When I look at the marbles now, I get kind of sad, you know? Maybe they'll make Juana happy."

Terrence recognized the dilemma posed by this unique gift. With theft of flowers from gravesites for other gravesites an occasional and frustrating occurrence, he conceded the strong possibility of someone snatching the marbles. He planned to hide the pouch under his bouquet today, retrieve it on Monday, and keep it in a drawer at home. Leaving two, maybe three of the small, round objects on Juana's grave seemed like a safe bet to go unnoticed, and if someone did take off with them, he could always bring some more. Extending his hand for the pouch, Terrence saw Nigel's eyes moistening and recognized the significance of this kid's offering. At that moment, the magnitude of his small gift meant more than a thousand bouquets of pink roses.

"She always liked playing marbles with you, Nigel," he told him. "And if they can somehow make her happy, that's all that matters."

***

Kneeling, Terrence stared at Juana's grave without any attempt to hold back his tears.

"Happy birthday, Juana," he said, placing the roses in the center. Emotionally drained from the nagging guilt over his inability to help her when she needed him most, Terrence remained silent for several minutes, allowing the calming, temperate breeze to sift through his hair and caress his face.

"Last night, I was looking at pictures of our trip to

Hawaii," he told her. "My favorite one is you blowing out the candles on your birthday cake with a big ol' margarita in your hand. You looked so happy." Terrence chuckled. "We had us a time, lady." A deep sigh followed the disappearance of his smile. "That was almost four long years ago, back when you could see that beautiful blue ocean and those amazing sunsets." Gazing skyward, his eyes sweeping across the cloudless sky in reminiscence, Terrence returned his focus to Juana's grave before leaning to the side to retrieve the pouch from his jacket pocket.

"I've got a surprise for you," he said. "A friend of yours asked me to give you a birthday present."

Terrence untied the string that sealed the pouch, preparing to remove a few of the marbles but still leaving most of them inside.

"Nigel wants you to have his marbles," he told her. "But you know the way it works. I can't just leave the whole pouch here, right? Somebody will decide they want them, and then it's goodbye, marbles. Don't worry, though; the boy won't find out. I'll leave the pouch under the flowers today, and on Monday, I'll come back for it. But I'll leave you a few under some dirt where nobody will notice. That way, they'll be yours forever."

Leaving the pouch unsealed, Terrence concealed it under the pink blooms of the roses before rising to his feet.

"I'll be right back," he told her. "It's a lovely Saturday to walk around and enjoy the weather. I know that's what you would tell me to do."

Moving past the Levy graves, Terrence identified the remains of what appeared to be scorched black feathers scattered in the area. Remembering what Francisco told him about finding several dead and apparently burned crows, he realized those feathers weren't there during his visit to Juana last Wednesday.

"Weird," he said, speaking as if someone stood next to him. "Must have happened again over the last few days."

Brushing the thought aside, Terrence strolled along a nearby walking path for several minutes, passing a man, a woman, and two kids at one grave and two men at another. With the thousands of occasions witnessing such scenes, sharing the weight of their grief seemed more impactful now. Even a bit communal. He turned around to go back.

Gazing down on Juana's recently installed marker, Terrence suddenly felt a series of jolts under his feet, causing him to lose balance and stumble back. With his apprehension now centered on the impending possibility of a bigger earthquake, Terrence looked toward the people he'd passed a couple of minutes before to gauge their reaction. Surprised, he didn't understand their complete nonchalance, acting as if they didn't feel any shaking at all.

"Did you feel that one, Juana?" he asked. "Not long but strong."

In another few seconds, the ground beneath his feet started shaking again, not with the same intensity but for a longer period. This time, while the quaking continued, Terrence looked at the visitors again, amazed that they remained unfazed. Holding his gaze until the earthquake ended, he shook his head before lowering his eyes again.

What happened next was something that would remain in the forefront of his memory for the rest of his life..

In a slow, unexplainable movement that seemed like something from a drug-induced dream, the bouquet of roses started rolling over multiple times, leaving the previously hidden pouch fully exposed on the grave. A few moments later, the black and white marbles started working their way out from the untied pouch, away from the other colored marbles, heading toward the center of the grave like ants toward a mound of sugar.

"What the…" he mumbled.

Terrence continued watching in hypnotic fascination as the marbles proceeded to move in different directions until finally stopping, leaving a formation of three pairs of evenly spaced vertical rows of three and horizontal rows of two. Some of the same black and white ones were grouped together, other times separated. Despite knowing nobody else witnessed what he just saw, Terrence looked around anyway, feeling an uneasy isolation as his thoughts staggered forth in confusion.

This is impossible. What the hell just happened? Am I losing my mind?

An unanticipated weakness overcame him as he attempted to suppress a sudden lightheadedness. Dropping to one knee, he stared at the marbles again before closing his eyes and taking deep, slow breaths. The pleasant July day now seemed chilly, as if the temperature had dropped twenty degrees over the last few minutes. His uncertainty over what just occurred made him start doubting himself and he wanted to get home. He needed to get home.

"What just happened, Juana?" he said, rubbing a hand across his eyes. "Am I all right?"

Reaching out to collect the marbles, he stopped and pulled his hand away as if touching a hot stove.

"I need to get a picture of this," he said, speaking aloud again as if to someone nearby.

Removing the phone from his pocket, Terrence stood and took the photo before gathering the marbles and placing them back in the small white bag. Tightening the string to secure the contents, he got down on both knees, leaned forward, and brought his fingers to his lips before placing one hand on the soil.

"I hope God remembers it's your birthday, Juana," he said, whispering, his eyes watery. "And tell him you like your margaritas with crushed ice and a salted rim."

CHAPTER ELEVEN
THE FIRST COMMUNICATION

A man who usually preferred wine or beer rather than the heavier stuff, on occasion, Terrence treated himself to a glass of bourbon on ice. After his experience in the cemetery, and on Juana's birthday of all days, a first glass leading to a second one seemed like a strong possibility. Halfway through the first drink, as he sat staring at the photo on his phone, he pondered the idea of sharing the story with, perhaps, Andrew but decided against it.

"Lucky to get my job back," he said to himself. "A damn sure-fire way to lose it again."

Studying the picture, Terrence repeatedly played the scene over in his mind between sips. Raising the glass to his lips again, his eyes drifted toward the table with the alphabet cards. The time now seemed proper to return them to their box, leaving the table clean for the couple of framed, sizable photos of the two of them he wanted to have made.

"But first," he murmured, staring into the amber-colored glass, "I'll finish this off and have another. It's been a crazy day."

With the second glass three quarters finished, Terrence retrieved the empty box from the closet, placing it on the floor by the table. Rattled and struggling for any explanation, he wanted his cell phone within hand's reach to continue examining the photo in the hope of reaching a sensible conclusion. Scrutinizing it again, he spoke aloud, repeating the same thoughts without deciphering a thing.

"The flowers kept turning over and stopped at the edge of the grave. There was just a light breeze, so that wasn't the reason. Then, the marbles did something impossible. Impossible. I mean, look at 'em, man. Like damn soldiers lined up for marching orders. Three groups of six and each group in two straight vertical rows—two on top, two in the middle, and two at the bottom." Shaking his head, he looked at the picture with as much bewilderment and disbelief as if seeing Santa and his reindeer flying overhead on Christmas Eve.

"What in God's name is going on?"

Terrence took a large sip but delayed swallowing. Feeling the comforting, cool liquor inside his mouth, he started contemplating his mental health—an issue he struggled with after his time served in the jungles of Vietnam. He'd smoked his share of weed in those days, but what he witnessed at the cemetery seemed like the result of taking some hallucinogenic drug—something he'd never had a desire to try.

"If I don't tell someone, I don't know what I'll do," he whispered. "I can't keep this inside. But who would ever believe me?"

Putting the phone on the table, Terrence plucked a

card from one of the piles and leaned over to place it back in the box—but not before looking at the raised outline of the object representing that letter. A necklace, designed to be recognized by tracing one's fingers around the jewelry's edges, meant that Terrence held the letter "N." Curious, he glanced at the letter's Braille combination near the upper left corner to see what it looked like. Within several life-changing seconds, Terrence's world flipped upside down, and his intended glimpse turned into a wide-eyed, unwavering stare.

Two vertical rows of three pairs, two on top, two in the middle, and two on the bottom, struck him like a hard slap. Rubbing his eyes with his forearm, he grasped the phone from the table and enlarged the third of the three marble formations, showing two black ones next to one another on top, a white and black one paired in the middle with the black on the right, and another white and black coupled on the bottom row, but this time with the black one on the left.

He double-checked. He triple-checked. He lost interest in his bourbon and regained immediate clear-headedness, leaving him awed by his discovery. The white-and-black-dotted pattern of the "N" on the alphabet card matched the white-and-black marble pattern from Juana's grave.

Clasping his hands and plopping his elbows on the table, Terrence closed his eyes and bowed his head, his heart beating fast from the apprehension of uncovering something beyond his comprehension.

"Lord," he said, looking upward, "I need to know what's happening. Is Juana speaking to me? Is she all right? Am I all right? Help me figure this out, Lord. Please, I need to know."

Terrence leaned back and took a deep breath before reaching for his phone. Spreading his thumb and forefinger to enlarge each of the two remaining unknown letters, he picked up several other cards before finding the second match—the letter "D."

"OK," he muttered, "'D''s the first letter and 'N''s the last. Will it be a word? Someone's initials?"

With four cards remaining, Terrence found the final letter— "A," the one with a lone black marble in the top row on the left.

"'D-A-N,'" he whispered. "Dan? Who's Dan? Dan McIntyre?"

Terrence knew one person named Dan, and Dan McIntyre had moved his headstone-making company to Nevada the previous year. Juana knew the man from holiday parties, but their relationship was nothing more than brief conversations of no memorable importance. Terrence's eyes narrowed, focusing his attention on the three letters from the phone photo. He nodded his head in encouragement, hoping for more to come.

"I don't know what any of it means, Juana," he said, speaking to the picture as if on a speakerphone. "But if you're really trying to talk to me this way, I'll drop the marbles off in the morning and pick 'em up before I go home." An unconfident, abbreviated chuckle followed. "As the saying goes, in lieu of flowers, right?"

CHAPTER TWELVE
RABBI MICHAEL FEINMAN

After conducting their interviews, taking their photos, and uploading the footage from the security camera showing the shadowy image of the perpetrator, the last of the television and newspaper reporters finally left to turn in their stories. Another anti-Semitic hate crime, this time a large swastika with the words "Hitler was right," was discovered early that morning on the wall outside a Boyle Heights synagogue. The congregation's rabbi, Michael Feinman, sat inside his office with his elbows on the desk and his chin in his cupped hands, exhausted from the long day's emotional toll.

Starting with that six a.m. phone call from his assistant, Sheldon, about what had transpired in the predawn hours, he spent much of the day answering questions from members of the media while alternately meeting with staff members to discuss the incident and fortifying security. For Michael, the most fatiguing aspect in all of this centered around the painful reality of anti-Semitism itself: Enough never seemed to be enough.

"Anti-semitism has been called the world's oldest hatred, and isn't that the truth," he muttered. "Even after thousands of years, no matter where it just never seems to end, does it?"

Marriages and bar mitzvahs brought him joy. Speaking before the congregation during Sabbath and the High Holy Day services instilled pride, but the ever-present storm cloud of anti-Semitism served as a constant detriment in maintaining his love of Jewish life. From the days of slavery under the pharaohs to the centuries of the diaspora and pogroms, ultimately taken to the extreme by the Holocaust, the continuing episodes of modern-day hatred of Jews left him with no other way to feel about the world and a Jew's place in it.

In a room made dim by the partial closure of his blinds, Michael immersed himself in necessary quiet time before the next act of business—listening to the numerous messages on his voice mail from members of the synagogue. He anticipated their apprehension over attending further services and, as the temple's rabbi, its leader, he needed to project strength, fearlessness, and resolve in standing up to another hostile act against the Jewish people. But the inner battle of emotions raging within him remained tethered to the events of history and the realities of the present.

From time immemorial, God always seemed to be fighting a perpetual battle against evil, and no words of reassurance uttered from a rabbi's pulpit could guarantee a brighter outcome. And that skeptical thought, one the honorable Rabbi Michael Feinman never intended to voice to anyone in the congregation, filled him with anguish.

Encouraging faith in God and hope for a better tomorrow remained his eternal rallying cry.

Michael looked at number sixteen on his answering machine, representing the message total awaiting him and expecting all of them to be about the defacing of the synagogue wall. Sitting back in his chair, preparing to return the first call, he pondered one more thought:

Maybe every religion's universal expectation that God will take care of everything all the time is asking too much, no matter how many prayers are said. Maybe evil wins out as much as it does because every God, no matter which one, is overworked and overwhelmed from what humanity has wrought.

***

Nibbling on a pizza turned cold after finishing his final call, Michael reached for his black-framed glasses after opening his laptop to review the security footage again. An ex-junior college point guard standing five-foot, ten inches tall, with broad shoulders, medium-length wavy black hair, a neatly cropped beard, and inquisitive large hazel eyes, today's events left this forty-two-year-old rabbi feeling like a man twice his age.

Hoping to find something previously unnoticed that might help, he paused the video at the moment the man's face turned toward the camera. Though a bit grainy, the distinct visibility of the man's mocking smile before his contemptible act sickened Michael to the core. Despite having watched the video several times that day, his level of anxiety remained as high with this viewing as the first one that morning. Reaching back to massage his left shoulder blade, burning from a stress knot that apparently planned to pitch a tent and stay for a while, he tilted his neck to the side for several seconds to stretch the muscle before dropping both hands on his lap.

"Don't keep doing this to yourself, Michael," he said loud enough to hear it again as an echo in his head.

Closing his laptop and removing his glasses, Michael leaned back in his chair, thinking of the last part of the conversation he had that morning with Detective Fernandez of the LAPD. As tense and fatiguing as the day turned out, Michael still produced a soft chuckle, recalling what the detective told him—especially the moving piece of optimism he needed reminding of.

"Let's hope you catch this guy real soon," Michael said. "There probably isn't a single member of my congregation who didn't lose members in their family tree to the Nazis. Some of those losses reached double digits, so acts like this are felt very deeply by us."

"What's that expression you Jewish people say, Rabbi Feinman?" Fernandez asked. "From your mouth to God's ears?"

Michael laughed.

"Exactly, Detective," he replied. "I couldn't have said it better myself."

"I've got to go now," Fernandez said. "I'll keep you updated on anything we discover that you should know. And I ask you to do the same."

Rising to his feet, Michael shook the detective's hand.

"Of course I will."

Fernandez nodded and looked Michael in the eye.

"I've seen too much hate and anger in my years on the

job," he told him. "More than I ever imagined when I first started training at the academy. But I still hold out hope for my kids and the world they'll inherit. What else is there but hope, right? We gotta hope."

Michael offered a small, tired smile. Small and tired, yes, but still a smile.

"I'll say again what I told you earlier, Detective," he replied. "I couldn't have said it better myself."

At the end of the day, preparing to leave and rubbing his palms in a circular motion over his bloodshot eyes, Michael glanced at a small, framed photo of his deceased grandparents, Heddy and Benjamin. The latter a Holocaust survivor, they were buried seven months apart at Evergreen Cemetery, located fifteen minutes away from the synagogue. At that moment, he acknowledged the reality of overlooking and even forgetting about this unremarkable black-and-white photograph on the small round table in the corner. In the face of the attention-grabbing activities of his office, how could a little picture like that compete?

Michael looked at his calendar for the next day. He expected his bimonthly eight a.m. temple activity meeting with Sheldon, Deborah, and Cantor Horowitz to last its usual hour to an hour and a half, leaving him free for a couple of hours until his afternoon appointments.

"It's been too long," he said to himself. "If I leave Evergreen by twelve, twelve-fifteen, I should be fine. I'll go there tomorrow."

Michael slid the laptop into his briefcase, straightened the stack of folders on his desk, and called his wife, Nina.

"How ya doing, babe?" she asked.

"I've had better days," he told her. "Can't wait to get home. I could use a nice glass of wine with another one on deck. If I don't make it back in time, kiss the kids good night for me and tell them Daddy loves 'em."

"I'm glad you're finally coming home," she said. "I was concerned about you when we talked today. You sounded so beat up. I wish I could have been there for you, knowing how much pain you're feeling over this."

"And fear, Nina," he added.

"Of course."

"How'd it go at the Children's Center today?" Michael asked, wanting to change the subject.

"Same answer as most days," Nina answered. "Tiring but so rewarding. To see how these children learn to handle their blindness, how they interact with the sighted ones, is so darn inspiring. And I'm so proud of our little Leah. She's becoming a little more independent in the classroom and starting to make some friends."

"That's great to hear," Michael said. "It was a blessing when Blind Children's Center offered you the job."

"I can say the same about you when the temple accepted your application for assistant Rabbi," Nina replied. "Now look at you, Rabbi Feinman. Only forty-two years old and head of your own congregation."

Yawning, Michael rubbed a hand across his face.

"Days like today make me wonder if I shouldn't have gone into my father's carpeting business," he said. "But you're right, even having to make the move from the Valley and be farther away from our friends, things turned out well for us."

"Getting Leah into Blind Children's Center was our

first priority," Nina said.

"Absolutely," Michael replied. "And we've both learned how to read Braille, so when she's ready to start reading, we'll be right there with her."

Nina chuckled.

"It took a long time and some frustrated cussing, but I think we both got the hang of it. You, especially. You picked it up a lot faster than I did. And now Leah will be good and ready before we know it."

Michael closed his eyes and smiled. Pinching the bridge of his nose and taking a deep breath, he held the air for several moments before releasing a drawn-out, audible exhale.

"I know what I'm good and ready for, Nina," he said. "To get this day over with. See you soon."

CHAPTER THIRTEEN
A WORD OF WARNING

"I told the crew to leave the marbles alone," Francisco said, leaning on his shovel. "They wanted to know why you're doing it, and I told them what you told me—your wife liked playing with them." Waiting for a response, Francisco didn't get one. "Hey, C.T., did you hear what I said?"

"What?" Terrence replied, reacting with a quick shake of his head. "Oh, sorry, Francisco. I'm thinking about something I need to do. Anyway, I heard what you said. Thanks for telling the crew, I appreciate it."

Lifting the handle to resume digging, Francisco looked at Terrence and patted his heart three times with a clenched hand.

"Whatever makes you feel good in your heart, C.T., that's all that matters."

Terrence walked away, his mind fighting a losing battle over keeping his thoughts on work rather than the pouch of marbles he placed on the grave that morning. He removed his cell phone to check the time.

"Eleven thirty-three," he whispered. "I'll go there at twelve."

***

The warm breeze greeted Michael with a caressing of his face and an invisible stroking of his hair, offering a comforting albeit bittersweet return to Evergreen Cemetery for his first visit in over a year. Standing before the graves of his Romanian grandparents, Grandma Heddy and Grandpa Ben, a catalog of various memories seemed to simultaneously open in his thoughts. Their small apartment on Normandy Avenue near downtown didn't have much to offer, but when Michael — Mikey, as he was called then, had his monthly sleepovers, they always seemed like a mini vacation from home. Grandpa Ben knew how much Mikey enjoyed those trips to the Farmers Market on Fairfax Avenue for a hamburger or pizza for lunch, followed by a walk through the grounds eating their delicious, gooey, saltwater taffy. For dinner, Grandma Heddy started off with either her homemade barley soup or chicken soup with matzo balls, sending those wonderful aromas wafting through the apartment and lasting so long that Michael could still smell them the next morning. Although he ate the sugary taffy that afternoon, Grandma Heddy somehow always found the time to bake cookies for dessert — with the stipulation that Mikey not tell his parents because they wouldn't approve.

Of the several sleepover memories Michael thought about as he faced their headstones, perhaps the one he valued most brought him back to those times when Grandma Heddy sang Romanian lullabies after he got into bed. And for some reason, despite not understanding the meaning of the words, he still remembered a particular one, "Cantec de Leagan," that was passed from one Romanian generation to the next over many years. Addressing Heddy's grave, Michael smiled at the memory.

"I'll always cherish those lullabies you sang to me, Grandma Heddy," he said. "Especially the one that starts off with, 'Hai Luluțu dormi un picu.'"

Michael chuckled. "Are you ready, Grandma? Feel free to join in."

Looking around with a bit of self-consciousness, Michael started singing in a soft, pleasant-sounding, mid-range voice.

"Hai Luluțu, dormi un picu…"

Wiping a rolling tear from his face as he sang the final words, "Ca al mamii pui," Michael said, "I pray you're resting in peace, Grandma, but this time it was your Mikey's turn to sing you the lullaby."

Looking at his watch, now reading 11:35, Michael debated whether to return to the office or to linger a bit longer to enjoy the pleasant weather. The sunshine and clear blue sky acted as an undisguised temptation and, deciding that another couple of hours in the office was worth the chance to spend more time outdoors, a stroll of these historic grounds seemed too enticing to pass up.

"Goodbye, Grandma Heddy," he said. "Goodbye, Grandpa Ben. I promise you I won't wait so long to visit next time. I miss you, and the memories you provided will always be a part of me."

Michael turned around and gazed out among the thousands of graves extending in every direction. Spotting a bank of trees in the distance, he figured they made a good turning point and headed in that direction. As he walked past the many markers, from ground level to small, mid-size to large, he observed the extensive patches of bare terrain dominating much of the grounds – in marked contrast to the days when rainy winters in Los Angeles were commonplace and verdant days of green grass surrounded the burial sites.

Many of the gravestones contained photos of the deceased, putting a face to the vital, meaningful, flesh-and-blood histories buried underneath. He felt a sense of wonder, even awe, recognizing that each of these many thousands of burial sites represented lives that experienced what we all do, the connective tissue of tales and time – love and heartbreak, joy and sorrow, successes and failures, laughter, and tears. Reading the names and birth and death dates, along with words or phrases of tribute carved into the headstones, Michael sensed a feeling of spiritual kinship to these Angelinos who preceded him, either from many years ago or who died during his own lifetime. But the ones that affected him the most were the infants, some of whom didn't even reach their first or second birthday. As a rabbi, the moments of attempting to offer comfort and healing with a congregant's loss of a child always fell far short in his mind, leaving him questioning God's reasons for taking a child from his parents – something he'd never fully accept as just another example of the unfairness of life.

Rounding a corner and nearing those groups of trees he spotted earlier, Michael caught site of a gravestone with what appeared to be marbles placed in some kind of design. Spotting something other than the usual flowers on a grave intrigued him, and after walking over for a closer inspection, the recognition of their black and white formation startled him.

"Oh my God," he whispered. "These marbles are Braille letters."

Michael speculated that the three letters he identified could be someone's initials because they didn't spell out a word. Reading the marker of a woman named Juana Covington, he felt a tinge of sadness over the recency of her passing, having occurred just weeks before. Michael wondered if perhaps this deceased woman had been blind and this was someone's way of leaving a message. Sweet as this gesture appeared, it struck Michael that if this woman was blind, and if her spirit existed in an afterlife, was she still blind?

Touched by the newness of Juana Covington's passing, Michael recited "El Malei Rachamim," a Jewish prayer for the soul of a person who died. Pausing for several moments after delivering the final words, he took another glance at the Braille lettering and the small bulky pouch with more marbles inside before starting his walk back to the car.

Removing the cell phone from his pocket, Michael saw that not as much time had passed as he originally thought, and at a few minutes before noon, he still had some extra time to enjoy the weather and continue with some overdue exercise. After sending a text to Sheldon, informing him what time he'd return, Michael decided to take a roundabout way back to his car, an alternate path that first led him in the direction of the Hollywood sign on Mount Lee, located in the Santa Monica Mountains northwest of the cemetery.

The luck of a steady, haze-clearing breeze provided a clear view of those nine, white, forty-five-foot corrugated steel letters. From Michael's vantage point, they didn't just stand as a landmark for the city of Hollywood, famous home of dreams and heartbreak, but also for the city of Los Angeles itself—the City of Angels, yes, but unfortunately, the City of Devils, too.

***

Having no appetite over his anxiety to see whether Juana had left more letters, Terrence eschewed the lunch truck and drove his car at twelve o'clock to the parking area closest to Juana's grave. Grabbing the box of cards from the back seat, he hurried over, a kaleidoscope of nerves and excitement tumbling together. When the grave appeared in view, and he spotted what he'd been hoping for, his heartbeat quickened along with his footsteps. The black and white marbles were out of their pouch and forming another three letters.

Resting on his knees beside the grave, Terrence fumbled through the box of alphabet cards, searching for the matching letters. The challenge and success of his discovery from the night before brought another feeling of exhilaration when he found one of the letters—an "E." After several more minutes, he uncovered the other two—an "R" and a "G." Without any possible three letter combination forming a word, the idea of someone's initials resurfaced as a consideration.

But why would Juana send initials again? he asked himself. Am I not seeing something?

Confused and frustrated, Terrence decided he needed some time to think things over, so a sandwich from the truck now seemed like a good idea to eat and sit and contemplate what these letters might mean. Snapping a photo of the marbles, he gathered them up and put them in the pouch.

"I've got to work late today, Juana," he said, "so I'll be back in the morning. I don't know what you're trying to tell me yet, but let's keep trying, all right?"

Turning to head back to his car, Terrence's legs buckled as the ground started shaking, stronger than the previous day and forcing him to drop to a knee. Releasing the pouch, he spread his ten fingers on the ground to wait out the shaking, looking like a track runner at the start of a race. In another few seconds, the shaking stopped. About fifty to sixty yards away, Terrence spotted a man standing and looking at him, seemingly oblivious to such a strong tremor ending moments before. Like those people from the other day, the man's behavior contradicted what a person's expected reaction should be moments after an earthquake.

A sudden realization occurred to him, leaving Terrence questioning his sanity. LA news shows always reported earthquakes, even the smaller ones he never felt, but as a person who watched the news every evening, he couldn't recall any mention being made of that previous one—strong enough to make him lose his balance. Why? Could it possibly be that the ground only shook near Juana's grave? Crazy as it seemed, it offered a viable explanation to his question about why he felt something while others around him apparently felt nothing. Was she trying to get his attention?

Making a slow, cautious rise to his feet, Terrence noticed the man he observed moments before coming toward him.

"Are you all right, sir?" Michael asked. "I saw you fall."

Terrence grimaced, but not from any pain. Feeling embarrassed at needing to drop to a knee, frustrated at the seemingly meaningless letters from Juana, and still unsure as to why this man didn't also feel an earthquake, he waited a moment to respond until regaining his composure.

"I'm OK, thank you," he answered. "I just stumbled over my own foot. Silly of me."

"Good to know," Michael said. Extending his hand, he introduced himself.

"I'm Rabbi Michael Feinman," he told him. "Head of Congregation B'nai Jacob over on Fairmount Street."

Terrence's eyes widened in surprise as a small smile appeared.

"A rabbi, huh?" he said, offering his hand. "I've seen some through the years here, of course, but never spoken to one like this before."

Michael chuckled. "Well, hopefully, I don't come across as anything other than a normal guy who happens to have a job as a rabbi," he replied.

"I guess you don't see people who look like me in that temple of yours," Terrence remarked.

"That's true," Michael said. "And being honest here, I welcome the chance to spread my wings a bit and talk with others outside my faith. And color. I don't get enough of that."

Terrence barked a short laugh.

"Mixing it up like that is something the world needs more of, rabbi," he said. "Sure, we got our differences, but guaranteed we got a lotta things in common, too. We just need to talk more to each other and find out, is all."

"Amen to that, sir," Michael replied. "And please, call me Michael."

"And call me Terrence," he responded. "Full name's

Terrence Covington."

At the mention of Terrence's last name, Michael took an inadvertent glance toward Juana's grave. Terrence noticed.

"My wife, Juana, is buried in that grave," he explained. "She died recently."

"I'm very sorry for your loss, Terrence."

"Me too, Michael," he said. "Me too."

Michael heard the strain in Terrence's voice, his low register slipping into a softer, slightly higher range as he finished speaking.

"Are you a religious man, Terrence?" he asked. "Sometimes God can be of great comfort."

"I'm a churchgoing man," he told him. "But that doesn't mean I always agree with what the Man above does."

"Just because you're a man of faith doesn't mean you're not allowed to have questions," Michael told him. "I'm a rabbi, and I'm no different. We're all left wondering about the bad stuff sometimes."

"I learned that the hard way in Vietnam, Michael," Terrence said. "When it comes to war, what's right, wrong, fair, unfair, whatever, it all becomes irrelevant. We were just trying to survive. After the things I saw and did, I brought those questions home with me on that plane."

"I hope you found the answers to bring you peace," Michael said.

Terrence's lower lip jutted outward as his eyes narrowed in a pensive expression.

"I've learned that finding peace in this world is like chasing a butterfly with a net," he told the rabbi. "It's hard to capture. It's elusive. But in those moments when you have it, you appreciate the beauty of it for all it's worth."

Terrence smiled and rubbed his hand across his face, leaving him with a sheepish expression. "Sorry for rambling on like that," he said.

"Are you kidding, Terrence?" Michael replied. "In my next sermon, I'm going to recite what you just said, giving credit to you, of course. Coming from a veteran, it puts a lot of our normal lives and complaints in perspective, and I think it can make for a real learning experience. Thank you for sharing that with me."

Terrence nodded in acknowledgment before bending down to pick up the marble pouch near his foot.

"I've got to get back to work, Michael," he said. "Thanks again for coming to see if I'm all right. I appreciate it."

At that moment, Michael realized how much he wanted to know the answer to the meaning of the marbles.

"Terrence, one question before you go, and if you don't want to tell me, I certainly understand," he said. "Before I saw you, I passed your wife's grave and couldn't help but notice the marbles in a certain pattern on the ground. My six-year-old daughter has severe visual impairment, and my wife and I have learned how to read Braille to help her. I don't think I'm mistaken about the three letters I saw spelled out with the black and white marbles. Am I right?"

Terrence stared at Michael, momentarily speechless.

"So you know how to read Braille?" he asked.

"I'm no expert," Michael told him, "but good enough to recognize the letter formations in your marbles. Do you also know Braille? Are you the one who placed them there like that?"

"Juana lost her eyesight the last few years of her life and studied Braille so she could read again," he explained. "She was a librarian, and reading was a big part of her life. She loved books. I learned a few letters from her, but that's it."

Terrence knew the next part of his answer needed to be a lie.

"So yeah, I placed the marbles there this morning. Just a little thing between Juana and me."

Michael smiled. "Well, then, I won't ask what the initials stand for," he said.

Terrence felt tempted to ask what letters the marbles spelled, but that would expose his lie. He'd have to wait until he got home.

Reaching into his pocket, Michael removed a leather business card holder and handed a card to Terrence.

"This chat brightened my day, Terrence, so thank you. I get so wrapped up in my work that I sometimes feel isolated from the outside world. You're a good man, and if you ever have the need to talk to someone, I'd be happy to meet you for a cup of coffee or lunch. If nothing else, it will give me a chance to do some of that 'mixing things up' you talked about earlier."

Terrence laughed as he placed the card in his wallet.

"A black man and a Jewish man having lunch together, huh? Guess we'll have to flip a coin between soul food and deli."

***

Enjoying the calming sensation of the hot mint tea he welcomed after dinner, Terrence sat in his chair thinking about the three letters he solved after he arrived home from work — R, E, and G. He wondered why Juana sent such a strong jolt that afternoon when new letters already showed, wishing he could have returned after work to give her another chance. But Anthony had informed him about a morning service the next day, and he needed Terrence to work overtime to complete maintenance repairs. Perhaps another message would show up tomorrow to make more sense of things.

Terrence also considered the possibility of the letters meaning nothing at all, just a humorous, heavenly game on Juana's part. If that was the case, it sure brought a whole new light to what happened when somebody died. Chuckling at the silly possibility while placing the cup on the table, Terrence started rubbing his hands on his face like a washcloth, his weary mind feeling the weight of the last forty-eight hours. Keeping his hands there, he remained motionless, enjoying the comforting feel of their warmth and the meditative sound of his breathing. His eyes remained closed as he pondered what he'd figured out thus far and where this might be leading.

Tired and feeling an ongoing sense of frustration over his continual cluelessness from the two photos, Terrence decided to fetch the box of Braille cards and remove the six already identified. He first placed the D, the A, and the N on the left side of the table and then the R, the E, and the G on the right, the second set of letters placed in order of discovery. He peered at both sets of letters, his arm propped up on the table as his open hand supported his head. Studying what lay before him with the determined focus of a chess master, Terrence's eyes darted back and forth as he sat wondering, contemplating, deciphering, and...

"Oh my God!"

The hair on the back of his neck bristled at the frightening realization of what he had just uncovered. A nervousness swept through his body at the sense of something unknown, unproven, yet somehow possible if Juana was truly sending a message. The letters from today were correct, but his mistake stemmed from placing those three cards in the wrong order on the table. Without a word spelled out by any combination of the three letters and still skeptical of the possibility of being someone's initials, the idea of placing them in the order found on Juana's grave seemed unnecessary.

Until now.

Bringing the six cards together in their proper order, Terrence now understood that Juana was, indeed, attempting to communicate with him — a message requiring two days to complete. The confirming realization that this had nothing to do with Dan McIntyre impacted him to the core in that staggering instant of discovery. Terrence stared at the word, reciting each letter in a daze of sudden comprehension, apprehension, and inexplicable fear.

"D, A, N, G, E, R."

CHAPTER FOURTEEN
FLIES

"You gonna eat with us, C.T.?" Francisco asked.

"No, not today," Terrence answered.

"What's the matter, man?" Francisco asked, smiling. "You don't like eating lunch with us macho Mexicans anymore? Been a long time."

Without waiting for Francisco's conversation with Terrence to end, the other three members of the landscape crew carried their wrapped food items and drinks from the food truck and headed toward the shade of a large pine tree about fifty feet from the entrance gate. Holding two cheese and bean enchiladas in one hand, with a can of Sprite in the other, Francisco waited for Terrence to pay for his grilled chicken sandwich and can of Coke before answering the question.

Terrence smiled and shook his head.

"I like you guys plenty," he said, "and I'll start eating with you again soon. Just spending some time at my wife's grave, getting used to things."

Three days had passed since his Monday evening

discovery of Juana's warning about something he had no understanding of, and Tuesday, Wednesday, and Thursday produced nothing. Terrence felt helpless, afraid of an unknown situation he couldn't figure out or attempt to prevent. So many levels of possibilities defined the word danger, from a simple reminder to get his brakes checked to some racist lunatic storming their church with an assault rifle. He needed more information. With each successive inactive day after that message, he repeated his routine—leaving the pouch of marbles in the morning, going there at lunchtime, and, if there was nothing to see, returning before he went home.

Clutching his sandwich in his left hand and cradling the box of cards with his right arm, Terrence nudged the car door closed with his hip before heading toward Juana's grave. Anticipation no longer fueled his curiosity, confronted as he was by the possibility the messages may have ended for good.

"Danger, Juana?" he asked, scanning the patchy clouded sky. "Really? You leave me with that?"

Terrence rounded the curb leading toward the gravesites, hoping for a message but preparing for another unopened pouch. Spotting the exposed black and white marbles no longer on the inactive list, he speed-walked the rest of the way, dropped to his knees, and studied the letters showing three on top and four underneath.

"Two lines this time, Juana," he said. "Did you spell out the whole word for me?"

Recognizing the "E" from before, he saw two more of them today, the second letter on top and the first letter below. Terrence placed the next deciphered letter, the "P," as the first letter of the first word on top and caught a break when the next letter he plucked from the box, the "T," turned out to be the final letter on top. Reining in his impatience to find that final unknown letter, he uttered a muted shout upon discovering the "V," with its three vertical black marbles on the left and two white, one black on the right.

Before taking a photo, he removed his pen and notepad.

"P, E, T on top," he said, writing and whispering simultaneously. "And E, V, on the bottom." Studying the letters, Terrence shook his head in frustration.

"This makes no sense, Juana," he complained. "But I learned something these last few days waiting for a message from you. Maybe you need more time to finish. So why don't I just leave the marbles in a neat little pile outside the pouch, and if you have more to say, I'll be here eating my lunch."

A few bites into his sandwich, as Terrence sat in a partial leaning position with his free arm supporting his weight, he felt the unmistakable movement of the ground. This quaking didn't match the intensity of the previous ones, but once he started feeling it, he leaped to his feet and waited, wondering what might follow. Watching the marbles start to move, he paused in nervous excitement, still awed by the reality of Juana communicating with him.

Two more letters showed on top and two more on the bottom. His increasing handling of the alphabet cards led Terrence to remember certain letters over others in addition to the "E." With one remaining letter on top, he realized what that last letter must be to complete the word or, in this case, the name.

"Peter," he said out loud, reading from the print on the notepad again. "Peter, who?"

Glancing toward the Levy headstones, he wondered about a possible connection.

"Peter Levy?"

Matching the third letter of the bottom row, a rush of heat spread though his neck and face in direct correlation to his increasing nervousness. The two black, four white marble setup, representing the letter "I," with its igloo diagram in the center of the card, signaled what the final letter must be.

Looking with a sense of dread at that "L," Terrence's thoughts clouded over from a combination of puzzlement and a sense of alarm, unable to think of anything else or derive any answers as he stared at Juana's new message.

PETER

EVIL

Terrence swiped away a couple of flies as he crouched low, staring at what this new marble formation spelled. Taking a photo, he shooed several more of the insects away from his face while scribbling on his notepad.

"What are you telling me, Juana?" he asked, his pleading tone conveying a growing desperation. "I don't understand. Are you talking about Peter Levy? That he was an evil man? He's dead, so why should that matter anymore?"

More flies descended on his ears and neck as he walked over to Levy's grave. Startled by the swarm of insects circling the headstone, he figured they must be a byproduct of whatever physical or odorous remains still lingered from those dead crows. Telling himself to check on this issue in the coming days, Terrence returned to Juana's grave, grimacing at the sight of his fly-infested chicken sandwich, smothered to a point of concealing the sandwich in a mass of buzzing black.

For over two more weeks, despite Terrence's daily marble routine, no further messages from Juana appeared. His growing disappointment sent him into an emotional funk despite the small consolation of the apparent disappearance of the nasty fly problem.

Like Juana's messages, however, those flies would return.

And so would Peter Levy.

CHAPTER FIFTEEN
FIRST

July 31, 2017 — one day before the seventy-fourth anniversary of Peter Levy's death

Walking from his car to deliver the marbles on the first day of the workweek on the last day of the month, Terrence heard a loud, disturbing buzzing coming from the area of the gravestones. Hurrying around the curb to see the reason for it, he halted in his tracks at the sight of the sickening scene before him. Mesmerized, he stared at Peter Levy's gravestone, now resembling a bee-covered hive but with flies instead. Not one inch of the gray marbled stone remained visible. Another cautious few steps brought him close enough to view numerous and sizable black spiders crawling in and around the grave. As the bitterness of acid reflux burned its way up into the back of his throat, Terrence fought back the urge to spew the oatmeal he'd eaten an hour before.

Moving with tentative steps toward Juana's grave, the maddening sound of the buzzing intensified his growing concern about the truth behind her messages. Hit by an unnerving realization that the unique and horrible deaths of the crows and the nauseating scene playing out at Levy's grave might be related, he fell to his knees and lowered his face.

"What in God's name is going on here, Juana?" he asked in fear-fueled anger. Hoping for some kind of sign, he dropped the pouch and rose to his feet.

"Tell me!"

An explosive yet brief shaking forced Terrence to open his stance and hold out his arms to maintain his balance. Returning his attention back toward the pouch, his eyes widened as the black and white marbles rolled out, moving faster than the previous times.

Unprepared for a marble reading, Terrence hurried to his car and retrieved the box of cards. Refusing to look at Peter Levy's grave and struggling to block out the hideous sound emanating from there, he waited for the completion of the message.

"Just one word?" he asked, looking at the four Braille letters. "Or one name? What's that going to tell me, Juana?"

The first letter showed a two-black, four-white combination producing a "K." He recognized the second letter from last time, an "I." The next two letters matched each other, and as Terrence rubbed his finger along the outline of the locomotive in the center of the card, he felt a gnawing fear in his gut of something unknown and, worse, unavoidable. At that moment, he wished he could be on a locomotive going somewhere, anywhere, away from whatever awaited him. The stillness of the marbles, objects intended for innocent fun, now represented a frightening warning about the looming of something sinister.

K I L L

"You need to tell me more. Please."

After ten minutes of inactivity, Terrence needed to start work. Returning at noon and disregarding the activity of the flies as much as possible, the adrenaline surge from seeing another message created a mad scramble with his hands searching for the three letters not seen before.

A U G

"A, U, G?" he said, reciting the letters. "August? Something's going to happen in August? When in August? Tomorrow?"

Reaching for the pouch, Terrence wanted to confirm a suspicion. Without knowing the total number of black or white marbles, he emptied the bag and discovered two remaining unused black ones but no additional white ones, meaning that the three letters chosen by Juana required all ten of the white ones and eight of the black.

Placing the two extra black marbles on the ground, he counted all the other colors and discovered that each of the other four, the red, the yellow, the blue, and the green, came in groups of ten.

Terrence now understood the limits behind completing the words and the reason for Juana's inability to finish her messages. The only way to create readable Braille letters without confusing him was to stick to the easily understood contrasts of black and white on which she modeled her spelling from the alphabet cards. But Terrence devised an idea to give her the chance to communicate more of her messages at one time.

"It doesn't just have to be the black and white ones, Juana," he told her. "If you need more than ten black marbles, start using the blues, and if you need more than ten white, start using the yellows. They're close enough."

From the time he arrived, the humidity and the otherworldly buzzing from the flies generated an increasing edginess and desire to get away from there. He removed a small cloth from his pocket and wiped the sweat from his forehead and the back of his neck.

"Unless you can tell me what day in August, I'll leave," he said. "I can't stay here much longer. I never thought I'd see anything to match the swarms of flies in the jungles over there, but what's going on at Peter's grave is something like I've never seen, and it's really getting to me. I don't know why it's happening, but I have a feeling that you do."

After waiting several more minutes without a response, Terrence told Juana what he always did during his noon visits—he'd be back at the end of the day. Returning after work and observing a four-letter word formation, Terrence felt a renewed optimism when he discovered her use of four blue marbles and four yellow ones in addition to the ten black and ten white.

"You heard me, Juana!" he shouted. "Now, help me figure this out."

In the now familiar grouped rows of three down and two across, he received the answer to his earlier question about what day in August. From the apparent urgency fueling her warnings, Terrence now stood on the precipice of facing the start of whatever Juana wanted him to know about. Freed from the limitation of the ten white and ten black marbles, the additional four blue and four yellow ones allowed her to write the complete word for Terrence to understand.

FIRST

"That's tomorrow," he whispered. "Oh my God, what the hell's going to happen tomorrow?"

CHAPTER SIXTEEN
UNGODLY

Per his usual early morning routine as landscape supervisor of the cemetery, Francisco arrived before the other three workers in his Ford Ranger pickup at five forty-five, an hour and fifteen minutes before the gates opened to the public and approximately fifteen minutes before dawn on this first day of August. The other crew members, Eduardo, Roberto, and Hector, started work at seven o'clock, bringing the landscape equipment in the flatbed of their own company vehicle.

Opening the gate with the key provided for the landscape company, Francisco drove his truck inside, got out, and relocked it. His focus this morning, like most, centered on the irrigation issues common to the grounds of such a large, old property dependent on an aging system in constant need of upgrading. Although the predominance of brown, weedy grass dominated much of the view, many other lawn areas still retained the green blades and healthy shrubbery sustained by Francisco's conscientious attention. Getting an early start with a forecast of temperatures in the triple digits justified his sunrise start time, and this morning, two broken irrigation valves needed replacing.

Francisco drove along the path with his windows down, enjoying the temporary comfort of the morning air coupled with the various chirping sounds emerging from the trees. Despite the gradual awakening of the sun, broad, tree-induced shadows maintained their embrace over much of the grounds, including the location of his first valve replacement requirement on the southeast side.

Francisco removed his jacket and exited the truck, first pausing to gaze at the seemingly endless rows of headstones of different heights, widths, and shades, but all joined in unison by their sole purpose of remembrance. Hardly a day passed that his working environment didn't give rise to thoughts about his own mortality. Surrounded by graves with every weed he cleared, shrub he trimmed, pipe he repaired, or valve he replaced, how could moments of wondering about what came next be avoided? A moral man, he sent money each month to his mother and sister in Zacatecas, remained loyal to his fiancée, and attended church every Sunday. The temptations from his earlier days, when drinking and chasing women defined his lifestyle, no longer appealed to him. At thirty-four years old, Francisco awoke each morning with a purpose and contentment.

Snapping back to attention for the business at hand, he removed his cap and proceeded to run his fingers through his thick black hair, anticipating another sweaty day. One deep breath later, he put his cap back on and moved toward the back of the truck to retrieve the valve, pipe parts, and tools. Time to get to work.

Twenty minutes into his digging of the hard, clay soil, Francisco stopped to retrieve a thermos of water from the truck. Leaning back against the door as he drank, he noticed what appeared to be a man dressed all in black standing over a grave to the left of the ones for Terrence and his deceased wife. The approximately hundred-yard distance from his present location prevented Francisco from getting a good look, but even from his faraway vantage point, he sensed something unusual about the man's solid attire. The clothes clung to his body as if painted on, without any normal cloth-rippled outline associated with a shirt or pair of pants.

Francisco wanted to take a picture for Terrence, curious to know if he recognized the man and if he knew how this person got inside the locked grounds. Realizing he needed a sharper, more identifiable shot, he moved closer before stopping to remove the phone from his pocket. Preparing to take the photo, Francisco reared back in surprise and lowered the phone, staring wide-eyed at something shocking. As the man turned to the side to move over another grave to the left, the unmistakable dangling movement from the genital area explained the reason why his clothes seemed so unusually tight.

He wasn't wearing any.

Francisco had never seen an African American man with skin as night-sky black as this one, making him consider the possibility of someone of any color, maybe a loco homeless person, painting himself in black from head to toe and wandering through the cemetery. This was Los Angeles, right? Realizing that his earlier thought about the man's clothes looking like they were painted on might be true after all, he hurried to click some pictures.

Lowering the camera but keeping the man in his sight, Francisco followed him as he moved back toward the grave where he originally stood. What he saw next left him motionless and staring transfixed at what was now occurring. Mounds of dirt spilled over both sides of the grave where the man stood, exposing a large, misshapen hole in the center. Within moments, something skeletal-looking, with a head, arms, and legs, appeared to rise from the grave. Francisco figured this must be some kind of magic trick, and it was by far the best he'd ever seen. The man proceeded to drop to the ground in a flat position facing the sky, and whatever that bony-looking thing was dropped on top of him in the same position. In the next few moments, the thing vanished.

Feeling shaken by the unexplainable and unsettling event that seemed so realistic, he couldn't tear his eyes away as the naked man rose to his feet, moved toward the open grave, and dropped to his knees. Leaning over the hole, the man now prevented Francisco from having a clear view of the activity occurring before him. Gathering the courage to move forward another few steps for a closer look, he watched the man remain in a kneeling position with his head lowered as if in prayer, moving his hands in a slow, repetitive, back-and-forth motion for three, maybe four minutes.

Rising to his feet, the painted man took several steps to the left, leaving a clear view for Francisco to see the entire grave looking as it did before, with every part of the soil appearing undisturbed. What he witnessed next terrified him, convincing Francisco that this person was no painted man performing a magic trick but rather something monstrous, something ungodly.

"Jesucristo!" he whimpered, crossing himself three times. "Jesucristo!"

CHAPTER SEVENTEEN
FRANCISCO'S FINAL DAY AT WORK

Peter Levy's return to life started as it ended that fateful August day, with his blackened, fire-ravaged flesh clinging like melted wax around his body. Standing over his burial site, released from the depths of his earthly confinement, he smiled in the knowledge that the grave no longer played a part in his future. The long wait now over, each revitalized moment of his spirit, his controlled spirit, was prepared to heed the call of its chosen purpose: to bring grief, pain, and, of course, death.

Peter turned to face the targeted location of his food source, eyeing the movement of the man in the distance. In a rapid sequence, his upper body leaned forward until both hands fell to the ground, landing fully extended on the dirt. In another few moments, Peter's entire body transformed into a muscular, four-legged, wolflike animal. His hands turned into paws, and coarse hair started layering his entire body and face. A shape-shifting metamorphosis of his facial features took effect as his jaws enlarged into a grotesque, over-sized shape, growing in length to accommodate teeth as sharp as spears for ripping skin from bone and limb from body.

Peter's resurrection represented a seventy-four-year proclamation fulfilled. But his reborn soul and flesh-forming ability needed restoring for everything required of him. The need to eat and drink dominated his senses, escalating a desire to satisfy his primal urges without further delay. Peter howled at the man looking at him before breaking into an immediate four-legged sprint.

***

Hurrying to gather his materials, Francisco grabbed his shovel and valve and tossed them in the back of the truck before returning to retrieve his box of irrigation parts. The brief metallic clanging of the slamming flatbed door echoed in the quiet of the cemetery. Feeling lightheaded and with legs turning wobbly, Francisco just wanted to substitute his sudden unsteadiness for the speed of his truck and drive away from there as fast as possible.

Never reaching the car door, Francisco's scream barely made it past his lips as Peter's teeth pierced the back of his neck. Swinging the body repeatedly against the truck like someone with a hatchet chopping down a tree, by the time Peter finished, Francisco's dead and broken body resembled a bloody, floppy scarecrow.

With this part of the undertaking accomplished, the necessary transition back to his blackened human form took place in order for Peter to remove Francisco's shirt, pants, and shoes. Placing the clothing on the hood of the truck, Peter looked down at his ravaged victim with drool oozing from his mouth. Resuming his wolflike animal form again, the time to satisfy his ravenous hunger had finally arrived.

***

Francisco Diaz lay face up in the dirt near his truck, the naked, ravaged, and almost bloodless body soon to be discovered as an indicator of his unthinkable and merciless end. After digesting much of the nourishing blood, bone, and flesh from this recent kill, Peter's capacity to transform into his original, unburned human form emerged, requiring several minutes to complete. With his fully fleshed features returning, every passing second brought him closer to resembling the handsome five-foot, eleven-inch man who boarded the B-24 fighter jet seventy-four years before.

From the quarter-moon scar on the underside of his chin resulting from a childhood bike accident to the broad shoulders, hairy chest, thick forearms, and river blue eyes he inherited from his father, and to the similarly shaped face, nose, and mouth he acquired from his mother, the man whose airman's photo adorned his gravestone now stood as the reincarnated Peter Levy, his physical conversion now finalized. In the silence of the cemetery, wearing the tight-fitting but passable clothes of Francisco Diaz, including the black polyester zippered jacket he retrieved from the passenger seat, Peter now looked like an ordinary guy ready to do ordinary things in the city. It would be in the quiet of the predawn hours, however, that he'd implement his long-awaited plans far removed from anything defined as ordinary.

Turning to look back at his burial site, he clasped his hands before rubbing them together, smiling in anticipation of the chaos to come, the terror to be unleashed, the human feasts to be savored.

CHAPTER EIGHTEEN
THE SEVENTY-FOURTH ANNIVERSARY

Card box in hand, Terrence exited his car at 7:30 that same morning, August 1, and immediately encountered a noticeable and disturbing sound — silence. The paradox of the peaceful cemetery surroundings triggering a prickly feeling in the back of his scalp didn't escape his attention. Straightening his shoulders, he turned his head upward to gaze at the crown of a majestic eucalyptus tree and took several deep, calming breaths. Feeling better prepared, he soon realized the relaxing breathing regimen he attempted couldn't be sustained with the shocking discovery at Peter Levy's gravesite.

Not one fly remained on the headstone, allowing Terrence to see the complete epitaph for the first time in several days. What he saw, or in this case didn't see, turned his ability to think clearly into a disappearing act. Unmoving and open-mouthed, he read the last line.

Airman Peter Levy
8th Air Force 44th Bomb Group

August 1, 1920–

The death date had disappeared.

Kneeling on the ground after hurrying to Juana's grave, Terrence threw the pouch down as his questions shot forth in a rapid-fire manner.

"What happened to Peter Levy's headstone, Juana? How is that possible? Why do you say he's evil? What do you know about him? What's going to happen?"

The ground started shaking. Terrence stayed on his knees with his eyes glued on the marbles rolling from the pouch. Four blue ones joined the twenty blacks and whites as they headed toward their designated spots. When the movement stopped, Terrence lurched toward the box, searching for the first letter of the five now showing. The three black, three white marble combination turned out to be the "D," with the duck figure in the card's center. He didn't require a search for the second letter because of his familiarity with the "E." With his confirmation of the "V" as the third letter, having seen it from the previous message of "evil," Terrence stopped and dropped his head in despair. The remaining two letters didn't require a search.

"Juana," he said, his questioning tone coated in fear, "are you telling me that Peter Levy is...the devil?"

The cell phone rang in his pocket, shattering Terrence's focus from this nightmarish news. He saw Andrew's name on the caller ID.

"What's up, Andrew?" Terrence asked, his attention still focusing on the marbles.

A slight pause preceded the reply, and when Andrew

did speak, he sounded weak, like a man who was sick or in pain.

"C.T," he said, "I need you to come to my office immediately. Something…something terrible has happened."

"Tell me what…"

Before Terrence could finish his sentence, Andrew hung up. His limited, brusque reply revealed a side of Andrew that, in Terrence's mind, highlighted the urgency.

"You warned me, Juana," he said, pushing the marbles to a corner of the headstone as police sirens sounded their approach. "Now I hope, I pray, you can tell me what I can do to stop it."

Arriving at the office building, Terrence saw four police officers rushing back into their two cars. Alarm bells went off in his head when he saw Rodrigo, one of the landscape employees, joining them. Rodrigo appeared to be crying, and his slow, stiff gait made him look like a man walking the plank. When Terrence entered the office, he observed Hector and Roberto, two of the other three crew members, hunched over in a corner of the room, both alternately wiping their eyes with their heads hung low. They remained quiet and immobile, seemingly lost in their own thoughts. Terrence noticed Hector's lips moving as he made the sign of the cross several times. Andrew's Administrative Assistant, Ramona, noticeably absent from the room, had left her chair askew and far from the desk as if she'd hurried out of there.

As he proceeded to enter Andrew's office with a cautious, increasingly sick feeling, he glanced at Hector and Roberto again, growing panicky at the realization that Francisco was the one missing landscaper from the regular four-man crew. Terrence closed his eyes and whispered a prayer before entering.

Sitting slump-shouldered in his chair with his hands gripping his knees, Andrew appeared staggered, drained of emotion, with moist, red-rimmed eyes and offering nothing but a vacant stare. The immediate sight of this usually upbeat and outgoing man in such a tormented state gripped Terrence with fear. He hesitated, unsure what to do or say.

"Sit down, C.T.," Andrew said, his weary voice cracking.

Terrence approached with tentative steps before grabbing the chair to sit.

"Did something happen to Francisco?" he asked, needing to know.

Andrew glanced into Terrence's eyes for a moment before turning away. Biting his upper lip, his eyes narrowed as he stared across the room through an open window. With a slow, repetitive nod of his head, he answered the question.

"Yes," he whispered.

Neither man spoke until Andrew took a deep breath, rubbed a hand across his face, and turned his attention back to Terrence.

"He must have been attacked by a wild animal," Andrew explained. "Judging by what happened, probably more than one."

"Jesus," Terrence whispered.

"Rodrigo found him. He just left here with the police to bring them there. Ramona called me and was sobbing so hard I couldn't understand her. She's the one Rodrigo told. I got here as fast as I could and...and saw for myself. I wish I never had." Andrew lowered his head, covering his face with his hands as his shoulders shook with the sound of his muffled crying. Terrence waited in silence, clutching and unclutching his hands until Andrew regained enough composure to continue.

"His head, his body…Jesus, his flesh ripped apart…so many bite marks… everywhere."

Andrew looked away, a man staring at nothing but his own living nightmare.

Terrence closed his eyes, his stomach knotted in revulsion. But also fear. He thought of Juana's warning and now realized that something otherworldly, something unimaginable, was now among them and must be stopped.

If possible.

"What I saw will haunt me forever," Andrew said, his hushed voice causing Terrence to lean closer. "The brutality is unimaginable. And to be left like that with nothing but damn flies all over him? Horrible, just so horrible."

Closing his eyes, Andrew shook his head before opening them again and taking another deep breath.

"That poor man. Jesus, what happened out there?"

At the mention of flies, the image of Peter Levy's headstone surged to the front of Terrence's mind.

"I can't…I can't explain why, how, any animal around here could be that vicious. We have coyotes, sure, but they don't attack humans like this." Andrew looked at Terrence, tilting his head with a puzzled expression on his face. "And there's one more thing I don't understand. Francisco was found wearing nothing but his underwear and socks. An animal isn't going to do that. It makes no sense. But nothing human could have done what I saw."

Furrowing his eyebrows, Andrew sat back and looked away, appearing as if he might start crying again. He offered Terrence a sad, weary smile.

"Please go now, C.T.," he said. "I just wanted to be the one to tell you."

***

The savage killing of Francisco Diaz by one or more animals was a feature story on the local news stations. Terrence shut off the television and his nightstand lamp after listening to a reporter interview Dragonfly, who explained that as he left his tent to "stretch his legs" just before sunrise, he saw a white man get on all fours and about a minute later leap over the cemetery wall, "like an animal would do, you know what I mean?"

The television camera zoomed in on Dragonfly's grizzled face.

"Leaped over the gate like some kind of coyote," he explained. "But it couldn't be no coyote because I swear it was a man I seen through the gate when he was inside, you know what I mean? That's how the bloodstains musta got on the sidewalk over there. He musta been the one killin' that gardener. He was actin' real crazy, runnin' around on all fours, makin' growling sounds, 'nuf to scare the life out of me, you know what I mean? I've known me some crazy people in my life, man, but this was the craziest damn thing I've ever seen. Ever, you know what I mean?"

Terrence knew from a previous conversation with the man that Dragonfly's "stretching" reference meant his need to urinate, so whatever he saw, his need to relieve himself at that time, got him a brief interview on the news.

"Juana," he said, his lonely voice carrying through the darkness, "if you can hear me, is there something I can do to help Peter Levy? He was a World War II airman fighting the Nazis and deserves to rest in peace. Maybe there's a way to lead him back to who he really was. Please, Juana, please, if you can, send me a message. Tell me what to do."

CHAPTER NINETEEN
EVERLASTING ABHORRENCE

Between maintaining the secretive shock over Juana sending messages from the grave, coupled with the unsolvable warnings they contained, Terrence's emotional turmoil sometimes seemed too much to bear. His simultaneous understanding behind knowing something murderous and evil was out there, but not understanding what it was created a desire to seek a calming presence. The workweek prevented him from talking with his pastor at church, located ten miles away near his home in South Pasadena, so Terrence decided to call Michael and take him up on his offer of lunch.

"I love working at the cemetery, Michael," he said, "but sometimes it's nice to get away and talk about things other than what I do here. I'll work some OT, so I won't have to be back too soon."

"And I'll do the same, Terrence. Got any lunch ideas?"

Both men laughed at the decision to meet at a popular Mexican restaurant, bypassing either a soul food or a deli option but agreeing on the convenience of the halfway spot for both. They chose to sit inside on this ninety-four-degree day, the air-conditioning offering a comfortable respite for Terrence to enjoy a couple of beef and chili tacos and Michael to eat his chicken, bean, and avocado burrito.

After a brief reference to the summer heat, the conversation turned to the Boys of Summer, the LA Dodgers, with the discovery that each shared a love for the team.

"Even when they were still in Brooklyn, my father became a big Dodgers fan because of Jackie Robinson," Terrence told him. "When they moved to LA, man, that sealed the deal. During the baseball season, Vin Scully's voice was our summer soundtrack. Those 60s teams, with Koufax, Wills, Drysdale, the Davises, yeah, that got me hooked. I was shipped off to Vietnam in February of '71, and following the Dodgers that summer helped me through some tough times."

"I obviously can't imagine what you went through over there, but it goes to show that sports can sometimes be real therapeutic," Michael said. "You mentioned Sandy Koufax. I'm pretty sure that every Jewish person who follows the Dodgers and knows anything about their history is aware of the time when he skipped the opening game of the '65 World Series against the Twins because it fell on Yom Kippur. My parents told me that it was big news back then."

Chuckling, Terrence shook his head.

"Don't have to be a Jewish person to know about that one, Michael," he replied. "Just like you don't have to be black to know about Jackie Robinson."

Michael laughed. "Touché, Terrence."

"Too bad Koufax's elbow blew out," Terrence said. "Right in his prime, too. That man was so dominant, he could have won a lot more games."

"His autobiography is a great read," Michael replied. "I'd be happy to lend it to you if you're interested. It holds a prominent place on my office bookshelf."

"Sure, why not?" Terrence answered. "I don't read enough, and that sounds like one I'd like. Maybe I'll come by the temple one of these days and get it from you."

"Either that or I'll bring it to you," Michael told him.

The conversation moved on to a discussion about the bond they shared with the blindness of a loved one, their mutual interest in jazz, their favorite television shows, and their opinions about different comedians. An hour later, aware of the time and knowing they each needed to get back to work, Terrence felt a sudden urge to ask Michael, a rabbi, a couple of spiritual questions gnawing in his gut.

"Do the Jewish people believe in life after death?"

Michael leaned back in his chair, raising his eyebrows with a surprised expression.

"That's a heck of a switch," he replied. "From Robin Williams to a discussion about life after death?"

Terrence reacted with a nervous smile, wondering if this kind of question might not be an appropriate thing to ask a rabbi.

"Like other cultures, Jews can be opinionated about many things," Michael said. "What happens after we die is certainly one of them. Disagreements have always existed. You can go all the way back to the Book of Daniel, for example, where it talks about how some who have died will awake to eternal life, while others might be judged as unworthy of that and face the consequences— 'everlasting abhorrence,' as they call it."

Terrence's eyes widened, and he looked at Michael in a discomforting silence. "Everlasting abhorrence?" he repeated. "You mean Hell? The Devil?"

"That's one school of thought, but not mine," Michael said. "I'm of the belief that an immortal spirit exists, and somehow, some way, what we do with our lives determines our fate. Do unto others, right? I think the Golden Rule is the easiest, most surefire instruction guide there is for safeguarding your soul."

Terrence hung his head, contemplating the difference in Michael's two answers and feeling no better about a fifty-fifty proposition.

"How about you?" Michael asked. "I'm thinking you wanted to know my answer because you have your own thoughts on the matter."

Terrence looked at Michael, his lips tightening as he thought about Juana.

"I don't know what I think right now," he said. "But if what you say about the Golden Rule is true, I feel good about the chances for Juana's soul. She was the kindest, most giving person I ever knew."

Michael reached out and patted Terrence's arm.

"Easy for me to believe she'll rest in peace, Terrence," he said. "Just by looking at you, I can tell how good a person she must have been."

Michael glanced at his watch. "I've got to get back," he said.

"Yeah, me too," Terrence replied. "But I'll admit to you that the other thing you said about the 'everlasting abhorrence' is bothering me. I pray it's not true."

"I don't believe in the idea of a Devil surrounded by flames and holding a pitchfork," Michael said. "But if the souls of mass murderers share the same playground as Juana or my loving grandparents, who are also buried at Evergreen, it sure wouldn't seem right, would it? Like a kind of betrayal to everyone striving to live the right way, past, present, and future."

Palms facing skyward with a look of resignation, Terrence shrugged. "And when our day comes," he said, "we'll find out who's on that playground."

Smiling, Michael nodded.

"None of us know for certain what happens after someone dies, but that sure doesn't stop people from having theories, does it? I'm a lot more inclined to believe in the existence of a peaceful afterlife without the need to also believe there has to be an opposite to that."

***

At the end of the workday, Terrence followed his daily routine of driving to the parking area near Juana's grave in the hope of receiving a new message. On rare occasions during that late afternoon to early evening time, other people visiting gravesites in the area showed up and parked along the same side of the pathway as him. Still, the sight of the white Subaru Legacy in the usually vacant area got his attention, knowing he may not be alone.

Rounding the corner and moving past the blanket of dry, serrated leaves dropped from a nearby oak tree, Terrence came to an immediate stop when Juana's grave came into view. The sight of Nigel and Krissy caught him completely off guard. Krissy stood looking down at Nigel as he kneeled over the grave, collecting marbles and putting them back in the pouch.

"Oh no, no," he whispered.

Krissy turned around and offered a brief wave of her hand.

"Hi, Terrence," she said.

Terrence's body stiffened as he moved with a forced smile toward the two of them.

"Hey, Terrence," Nigel said, rising to his feet with the full pouch now tied. "Somebody must have opened the pouch and played a game because all the black and white marbles were in some weird pattern. There were a few blues, too, but no greens, yellows, or reds. Don't worry, though, nobody stole any. All sixty of 'em are still here. I know 'cause I checked."

Terrence swallowed hard.

"Thank you, Nigel," he said.

"We've been wanting to come back and pay our respects," Krissy said.

Terrence retained his smile despite the weight of his secret dragging him down.

"I think it's wonderful that you both wanted to come here," he said. "It means a lot. I really appreciate it, and believe me, so does Juana."

"Nigel always looked forward to playing marbles with her," Krissy told him, her voice breaking. "And I really enjoyed styling her hair. We shared some good laughs." Krissy wiped away a tear. "Juana was a beautiful lady, Terrence."

Attempting to fight back his own tears, Nigel handed over the pouch, his eyes moistening and his lips squeezing together. At that moment, nothing meant more to Terrence than this young boy's memories of his time with Juana.

Watching Krissy and Nigel walk away, he waited for them to round the corner and disappear before opening the pouch and placing it back on the grave.

"Juana, can you do it again? Please, send it again."

Terrence waited and pleaded for another fifteen minutes before giving up. Removing the pouch and retying the string, he placed the marbles in his pocket.

"I'll be back as always, Juana," he said. "Maybe tomorrow, OK?"

CHAPTER TWENTY
SEEDS AND ROOTS

Zipping up his jacket in the chilly predawn darkness, Chef Kenji Yoshida strolled toward his Honda Civic, parked in the driveway of his house on San Pedro Street in Little Tokyo. The pale yellow vapor from the streetlight on the corner offered just enough visibility to open his trunk and inspect the linings of the empty containers in preparation for purchasing and packing that morning's haul from the market. Shutting the trunk as the sound penetrated the silence like a single drumbeat, Yoshida turned his head toward another sound — a sudden yet muted rustling coming from the other side of the shrubbery separating his house from his neighbor's. Pausing for several moments without seeing or hearing anything further, he shrugged and approached his car door. They were the final steps of Yoshida's life.

In a matter of moments after the murder, as the man lay sprawled between his car and the bushes, Peter's claws dug into the passenger-side door next to the body and scratched the white supremacist numerical symbol of 100 percent before moving to the hood and doing it again.

After finishing what he set out to do and at a speed unable to be reached by any other four-legged creature, Peter hurried from Little Tokyo for the three-mile return to Evergreen Cemetery. Arriving within minutes with his clothes clenched inside the elongated rows of his nearly three-inch teeth, he leaped over the gate and climbed out of sight to the top of a sixty-foot queen palm tree, ascending the trunk as easily as if gravity worked in reverse. Hiding within the cascading leafy fronds, Peter waited, planning his next idea until killing time rang its death knell again the following night.

***

A devout Muslim and student at USC studying online for his master's degree in global health, Amir prayed daily at home and three times per week at the mosque on San Julian Street. Open twenty-four hours, the mosque offered Amir the opportunity to visit and pray at night after his studies, providing a peaceful setting for comforting his mind and communicating with Allah. With Allah's help, he believed in his ability to fulfill his future goal of helping sick people in poor countries, perhaps even his homeland of Lebanon.

Nearing midnight, Amir rose to leave, moving silently toward the exit doors on the way to his car, parked a half block up the street. The solitude of the late hour in the otherwise busy industrial pocket of downtown provided the chance for Amir to reflect on his prayers and what school assignments awaited him the next day. With an occasional ineffective streetlight protruding from a telephone pole, most of which didn't have lights at all, the slight buzzing sound from the overhanging east-west, north-south crisscrossing wires offered the one indication of active human life other than the echo of his footsteps. In another few moments, a sudden, indecipherable noise brought an immediate end to the silence. And to Amir's life.

Through social media sites and television interviews, the miniature Israeli flag found in the hand of a savagely murdered Muslim man stirred bitter controversy and threats of retaliation from angry voices of the Muslim community throughout Los Angeles and the rest of the country, with demonstrations occurring on college campuses and in downtown areas of Los Angeles, Philadelphia, New York, Washington, DC, Boston, Atlanta, Houston, Chicago, Detroit, Dallas, and San Francisco. Mosque and synagogue attendance brimmed with the worried, the enraged, the curious, and the prayerful. Rabbis and imams throughout America encouraged dialogue and peace, asking everyone to let the police do their job and capture the sadistic perpetrator before passing judgment. What happened a week later, however, ushered in a new dynamic to the ongoing story.

***

All the residents in the lunchroom at the LA Jewish senior center sang "For He's a Jolly Good Fellow" to Henry, the beloved manager and friend to all. His eyes moistening from gratitude, the going-away party left him feeling bittersweet over his soon-to-be-past and soon-to-be-future life. Henry's permanent late-night departure from LAX that night for his East Coast move to Portland, Maine, represented the end of twenty-six years of collecting rents, organizing activities, and consoling grieving hearts.

"We're going to miss you, Henry!" shouted Ruth.

"There will never be another like you!" Arnold cried out.

"Marry me, Henry!" Abigail yelled.

Henry had anticipated this day, expecting it to come sooner rather than later. But his daughter-in-law's difficulty in conceiving finally turned into a success story with the birth of two twin grandkids and a chance to become a full-time grandpa. With the passing of his wife four years before and his daughter married and living in England, Henry carried on alone. Now, he looked forward to joining his son, his daughter-in-law, and their newly extended family. This new phase of his life offered potential and promise.

Reserving a taxi to pick him up in an hour, Henry left his suitcases in the quiet of the lobby and walked through the building toward the back exit doors. Stepping outside in a section next to the visitors' parking area, Henry wanted to make a final inspection of the storage facility in the corner of the lot. Strong, safe lighting flooded the area leading to the roomy, box-sized container, allowing Henry to find the string for the light switch without a problem.

With the overhead tubular neon light shining down, Henry gazed at the tools, brushes, irrigation parts, and other maintenance items representing a history of repair work and memories. The paint cans lining the bottom shelves, some still full, others half to near empty, reminded him of his successful efforts to convince the owner to go with the colors Henry chose for the dining room and library rather than the questionable ones originally requested. He chuckled at the recollection, recalling the owner's fondness for red and wondering how on earth that crazy notion could have been considered for those rooms. Within a few moments, however, the owner's preference for red found its way into portions of the storage room.

Blood red.

The hand-painted black letters on the wall greeted the police as soon as they entered the small doorway: Allahu Akbar. God is great. Within another twenty-four hours, after the explosion of the story on social media, and exacerbated by the continual television and newspaper reporting, the Jewish and Muslim communities throughout the country remained on high alert, bracing for possible trouble. Big trouble.

***

On an airless, smoggy Saturday afternoon teeming with the sounds of chatter and car engines, Peter strolled among the living in Boyle Heights, not giving anyone a reason to look twice at this nice-looking, young Caucasian man sixteen days removed from the grave. Scanning the areas for future opportunities, he surveyed various locations that seemed promising in their ability to provide chances for targeting humans still active in the late-night hours: restaurants, tattoo parlors, smoke shops, bakeries, bars, convenience stores, churches, music stores, coffee shops, liquor stores, gas stations, parks, and perhaps other venues he might discover along the way.

With the strength gained from the flesh-and-blood enrichment of his first two victims—the second being a sanitation worker in an alley behind a fast-food restaurant— the third victim, a Japanese American sushi chef, got off easy. Without the type of blood draining, flesh-ripping ending given to the other two victims, when the man approached his car for a four a.m. drive to the downtown fish market, Peter granted him a simple neck breaking — killing him instantly for the sole purpose of instigating another hate crime to exacerbate fear and anxiety in the Asian community.

Other than the Jewish community, which Peter intended to target more than the others as an homage to mankind's enduring legacy of anti-Semitism, the other ethnicities, such as the Asian community, offered him the chance to simultaneously ignite and spread other fires. Fermenting distrust and divisiveness in his quest to bring mankind to its knees motivated Peter, inspiring him and giving him a reason to feel grateful for a second chance at life.

As the hunger within him started growing again, Peter anticipated the pleasure of someone else losing their life that night in a gruesome way, offering another opportunity to announce his arrival as a spirit reborn for dividing and conquering. A spirit created as an unstoppable architect for the construction of chaos.

"Helpless and hopeless for them," he whispered with a smile, "but happily ever after for me."

Passing a Mexican restaurant on First Street, Peter's loud, cackling laugh at his own whispered comment drew the attention of curious patrons sitting at outdoor tables. Thinking about what he left behind on the dead chef's hood and car door, how could he not help but laugh? Or the miniature Israeli flag he placed in that dead Muslim's hand? Or the Arabic expression of holiness he painted on the wall after killing that Jew? Replaying the murders in his mind, his craving for more devastation and destruction intensified.

Seeds planted and roots starting to grow, the

manipulation of humans never seemed easier.

CHAPTER TWENTY-ONE
HUMMINGBIRD'S DREAM

Hummingbird awoke on the edge of a vast field of yellow, orange, and purple flowers, their sunlit, colorful heads expanding far into the distance, bopping and swaying to the silent music orchestrated through the breeze. The stimulating aroma of gardenias, "nature's perfume," as she called them, wafted by without exposing their hiding place, but being close enough to smell, that was all that mattered. Inhaling deeply and slowly multiple times, she felt a lightheaded high from the intoxicating fragrance.

The sweet sounds of buzzing bees and the distant, rhythmic gurgle of a river somewhere in the distance offered the only sounds around her, making Hummingbird's eyes fill with watery gratitude at the tranquility they offered. Remaining in her supine position, Hummingbird gazed up at the pastel blue sky, a blanket of comfort and magnificence extending in all directions. Focusing again on the sound of the river, she felt it beckoning her, enticing her, and directing her where to go.

Removing her shoes and standing, Hummingbird reveled in the soft, powdery feeling of the soil beneath her bare feet. Following the lapping of the rushing water, each footstep offered a sensual sensation of comfort the likes of which Hummingbird had never imagined. The splashing of the river remained in the distance, but the sound continued to grow louder, bringing her closer to satisfying her desire to drink from the cold, refreshing water. Maybe she'd even dare to go skinny-dipping if it was deep enough.

Hummingbird didn't remember how or when she got here, but she knew for certain it was where she wanted to be — far away from the drunkard, the molester, the abuser. Far away from her father.

Maybe she'd made a wish that somehow came true. Maybe God, or whatever you'd call a kind, compassionate universal power, took pity on her and waved his or her all-powerful magic wand to protect Hummingbird from further harm. The thought of that possibility regenerated her tears and she needed to stop and sit for a while to contemplate how she got so lucky. Luck had never befriended Hummingbird before. A victim of a violent, loveless family, she felt fortunate to survive. Now, after going to sleep in the unsettling darkness of a small, tattered tent on a dangerous city street, she awoke to a fantasy world of colorful flowers, exhilarating gardenias, a soft blue sky, and the enchanting sound of a river. Maybe this was Heaven, but qualifying as one of the lucky ones to make it there would run contrary to anything Hummingbird had experienced before. With skepticism prevailing, she wasn't quite ready to accept an answer having anything to do with luck just yet.

"Get up, girl," she said. "Whatever this place is, let's go find that river."

The winding path toward the happy, sloshing sound veered through the seemingly innumerable flowers, now offering even more variation of colors than she first saw upon waking. Stopping on occasion here and there to touch them and bring them close to her face, Hummingbird started to notice that the nearer she got to the increasing volume of the river, the taller they grew, eventually dwarfing her as if in a cornfield.

Brushing aside the final few rows of flowers, Hummingbird stopped and stared in disbelieving delight when she arrived at a free-flowing, shimmering blue river deep and wide enough to drink from and take that daring skinny-dip. Approaching the riverbank with a mixture of excitement and awe, she knelt low and extended an arm to bring a cupped hand of water to her mouth. Closing her eyes in adulation, she embraced the water's refreshing journey, from the temporary lingering in her throat to the euphoria of an icy explosion into her stomach. In Hummingbird's entire life, nothing ever tasted so good.

Rising to her feet in preparation for that naked swim, Hummingbird stared at the water in confusion as the clear blue color started darkening and changing its tint. A sudden awareness of the increasing shadows enveloping the entire area brought her attention skyward. The pretty sky's previous blue color now grew increasingly dark, a fiery reddish-black threatening something dangerous. As her gaze moved downward, Hummingbird felt a sudden destabilizing sensation overtake her senses when she looked at the flowers, now seeming like colorless giants peering down on her in doomy judgment.

Recognizing the need to leave, Hummingbird wanted to savor the delicious river water once more, but when she turned back for that final drink, her scream pierced the silence—soundless now from the disappearance of any rushing water splashing against the rocks. The river now oozed rather than flowed, a slow, thick movement of crimson.

Hummingbird's breathing grew short as she struggled to contain the thumping of her racing heartbeat. Covering her face with both hands, she tried to regain control of her emotions by closing her eyes and concentrating on taking slow, deep breaths.

Calm down, she told herself. Calm down, girl. Calm down.

Believing she now had herself under control, Hummingbird's eyes remained closed, her hands staying in place until she felt ready to look at the river again.

"OK," she whispered. "I'm OK."

Taking one final deep breath, Hummingbird lowered her hands with a slow slide downward past her nose, mouth, and chin, keeping her eyes shut for several moments more. What she saw upon opening them made her scream again. Under a lava sky, the river now flowed in an undeniable movement of blood—a slow, sticky, metallic-smelling, meandering horror darker than before. Hummingbird took several steps backward, smothered by fear. Another scream, this one longer and higher-pitched, powered past her mouth as the head of a chuckling, bloody, bald-headed man emerged from the river.

"Come on in, Hummingbird," he said, his menacing voice enclosing her in a glacier. "The water feels great."

Panicked, Hummingbird spun around and started running back through the flower field until she lost the strength in her legs and dropped to her knees. Summoning the will to get up again, she found herself surrounded by bobbing images of the bloody man's crazed face, sneering and sinister, expanding like inflating balloons atop every flower stalk in sight. Watching in numb, muted terror and unable to move, her eyes darted back and forth as one balloon explosion after another created geysers of blood ascending high into the air like spewing volcanoes. Flattening herself on the ground, Hummingbird started clawing at the crimson wet soil to propel herself forward. The sudden sharp pain from a familiar object cut her fingers, drawing blood but also drawing strength. Grasping the handle, she wrapped her hand around the knife, leaped up, and charged toward the snarling man in the river.

CHAPTER TWENTY-TWO
DRAGONFLY'S NIGHTMARE

Dragonfly stared, dumbfounded, at the sight of the three murdered men standing in front of him. This couldn't be happening. The Hernandez brothers, two Dragonfly had killed and one who died while almost killing him, pointing in silence at the open and empty grave near his feet. In simultaneous motion, they turned their gazes back on him, savage expressions through the blazing hatred of bloodshot eyes and the vengeful determination of mouths pursed in anger. Three men representing the culmination of those tense Texas years spent persevering by his wits and uncanny ability to stay alive — even in fights where life or death added up to the only possible two outcomes.

His limbs felt heavy, almost to the point of paralysis, preventing his ability to get away or defend himself. Gone was his usual swagger, dismantling his self-confidence. He didn't want to go back to that life, didn't want to return to that same man from years ago.

***

Jessie, as Dragonfly was called then, started dealing drugs when he left home at age fourteen, fed up with his loveless, alcoholic parents. Treating their only child as some kind of mistake, as a burden rather than a son, created the need for him to fend for himself, and leaving home challenged that need. In order to survive, Jessie moved in and out of the worlds of drug dealing, gun selling, chop shops, cock fighting, and collecting money as an enforcer. Breaking bones and using a gun if forced to do so, Jessie delivered punishment to those unfortunate clients who didn't pay their debt in time to his drug-and gun-dealing bosses, Victor, Danny, and Eddie Hernandez.

Whatever it took to outlast the dangerous times, Jessie followed that path, and a man of his smarts and toughness might have established his own crime empire had it not been for his love of Gabriela. An undocumented Guatemalan immigrant, Gabriela struggled through the days and nights as a kidnapped victim forced to do the sexual bidding of the brothers when she wasn't cooking the meals or cleaning the house they shared.

Gabriela feared for her life if she didn't cooperate, and of the four men she saw every day, Jessie remained consistent as the one person who talked to her with respect and never laid a hand on her. He hated how the brothers treated her, but he needed the job, so he continued suppressing his disapproval and disgust. As time passed, however, Jessie's affection for Gabriela evolved into love, and after crossing that emotional bridge, he couldn't live with himself any longer in allowing this forced depravity to persist. Gabriela's desperation to escape ignited his own urgency to help her. If successful, a couple of bus tickets to faraway California seemed like a good idea. He always wanted to see the ocean.

Over a seven-day period, moving in and out of the house for work, Jessie stuffed pieces of Gabriela's clothing inside his pockets, hiding them in the fold-out bed they provided him for sleeping in a small room off the garage. Jessie also confiscated barbiturates — spread out over enough days to avoid suspicion and enough, so he thought, to drug the men into a heavy sleep.

The night of the planned escape, Gabriela's primary role involved mixing in enough of the sleeping powder with that night's heavily seasoned beef stew to send the men into a deep slumber. Jessie pretended to be sick and stayed in his room, while Gabriela remained in the kitchen during dinner, as she did every night. In the early morning hours, they'd hurry away, never to be seen again.

But the plan, like the barbiturates, didn't work.

At two a.m., after Jessie unlocked Gabriela's room to free her and the two of them started their quiet departure through the front door, Danny Hernandez's booming shout echoed through the shattered silence.

"What are you doing?"

With the door open, the darkness of the entryway now held enough visibility from the moonlit night for Jessie to see Danny reach for his gun on the table outside his bedroom. Without a moment's delay, Jessie grabbed the Smith & Wesson 9mm pistol from his waistband and fired several shots, driving Victor back with a bullet through the shoulder before connecting with two more into his chest.

Another shot rang out, grazing Gabriela and causing

her to clutch her shoulder in pain as her body slid down the wall to the floor. A second bullet just missed Jessie, whizzing past his head and shattering the window behind him on the right side of the door. Jessie dove into a darkened area behind a brown pleather armchair, and as Danny charged into the room ready to shoot again, he hesitated, first eyeing the wounded Gabriela on the floor before turning his head to the right, where a crouching Jessie hid. With those precious few seconds of delay on Danny's part, looking at Gabriela, Jessie raised up from his cover and fired a direct hit through Danny's head just as he turned and spotted Jessie.

Eddie Hernandez remained the sole brother still alive. Unable to see or hear him as expected, the unsettling nature of questioning the man's whereabouts worried Jessie as he rushed toward Gabriela, appearing to be in better shape than he first feared. With his gun held in a ready position, Jessie's eyes darted back and forth as he helped Gabriela get to her feet. Without any sight of Eddie, Jessie wondered if the heavy dose of barbiturates somehow affected him, unlike his brothers. His answer arrived as soon as they approached the open front door.

The surprise attack from Eddie's unanticipated appearance outside the door caused Jessie to fall back into the house and lose his grip on the gun, sending it hurtling into the darkness. Eddie's knife cut through a swath of skin on the left side of Jessie's face as he tackled him, causing a flaming lava sensation to spread over his cheek and into his mouth. As Eddie tried to finish the job and plunge his knife downward, Jessie grabbed Eddie's wrist and twisted it back with enough force to cause the knife to drop from his grip. Without the aid of a gun or knife, they rolled on the floor, fighting like two ravenous dogs over meat scraps until everything ended in an unexpected and explosive way.

Standing and sobbing, with a bloodied shoulder and an immobile arm dangling at her side, Gabriela looked at the fallen Eddie, now clutching his chest with one hand and holding the other out for mercy. Approaching him with the pistol pointed at his face, Gabriela stood over her wounded victim for several seconds before moving the barrel from Eddie's face to his crotch and emptying the chamber.

With the middle-of-the-night aid of a doctor paying back a favor from a death threat Jessie took care of, the two bloodied survivors received the care they needed and boarded a bus to California early that morning. Within a year's time, Gabriela realized how much she missed her family back home and returned to Guatemala. Jessie stayed in California, though miles from the ocean.

***

And now the Hernandez brothers stood before him, looking intent on revenge and making it clear that Dragonfly's time to die had come. Raising their arms to point toward the open grave again, they approached him as if preparing to push him in before coming to a sudden halt a foot away. Standing face-to-face with Dragonfly, their stale, pungent breath nauseating him and making him gag, they moved several steps back, shoulder to shoulder, with no space between the three of them. Looking at the men as they lowered their heads, their faces no longer able to be seen, Dragonfly's eyes narrowed in confusion, baffled by the sudden movement of their bodies seemingly melding together. Confused and feeling a fear he'd never known, he watched the three bodies turn into a single large one as all the thick, black hair from the remaining head started falling to the ground like a heavy rain.

Dragonfly gasped as the man slowly tilted his bald head upward. The faces of neither Victor, Danny, nor Eddie Hernandez no longer appeared, replaced by a frightening-looking man with pale, sickly skin and yellowish, rotting teeth as sharp as daggers. Dragonfly's breath fled from his lungs as the man started laughing—a howling, diabolical shriek of a laugh that frosted his blood. Immobilized by terror, Dragonfly stood helpless as the man sprung forward, his open, drooling mouth and snapping teeth signaling his intention and leading the way.

***

Bolting upright from his sleeping bag in the semidarkness of the tent, with the lights from the streetlamps filtering through the tattered nylon, Dragonfly rubbed his face in relief. The last nightmare he'd had must have been as a kid, but this one seemed so realistic. Looking over at Hummingbird, who appeared to be in a deep sleep, he listened as she started making strange sounds. But she often talked and moaned in the middle of the night, so he ignored it.

Feeling a strong need to urinate— "stretch his legs," as he referred to it—Dragonfly slipped out of his sleeping bag and eased his gangly frame from the tent. The crumbling cinder-block wall, once separating a small parking area from the street, provided a perfect hiding spot to take a leak, so he started heading there, shaking his head over the crazy nightmare still fresh in his thoughts. In a matter of seconds, however, while fully awake, Dragonfly came face-to-face with a real-life nightmare he could never have dreamed about.

***

Jolted awake by Dragonfly's screams, Hummingbird grabbed the handle of the knife she always slept with and rushed from the tent. Within that split second of recognition, seeing the monstrous, wolfish beast standing over her bloody, mutilated companion, it was either kill or be killed. Raising her knife and bellowing a full-throated scream, Hummingbird charged toward the snarling creature.

Anyway, without Dragonfly, life wasn't worth living.

CHAPTER TWENTY-THREE
THE LOSS OF TWO FRIENDS

Terrence's mounting disappointment and desperation over not receiving further messages from Juana for over two weeks caused him to struggle at work, often losing focus on the task at hand. Arriving at work each morning, he'd offer a plea to her before placing the pouch on her gravesite. Additional horrific killings by purported wolf attacks and a sudden rise in racial and religious-oriented murders dominated the local news cycle, but different as they seemed to be, Terrence wondered about the possibility of a connection. He believed Juana could provide the answer, but without any messages, he grew increasingly despondent.

Arriving at the cemetery that Tuesday morning, however, the information Terrence received poisoned his weakened spirit even further, sending his mind reeling into a state of deep sadness. Getting through the day in a haze of uselessness, he headed straight for the bourbon bottle when he returned home, turning on a news station in the hope of learning more about the barbaric murders of Hummingbird and Dragonfly.

Hearing further details, tears welled up, and nausea almost overtook him. The reporter's interview with the policeman describing his discovery of the two butchered bodies as he made his rounds in the neighborhood challenged Terrence's ability to maintain control of his emotions. Hummingbird's and Dragonfly's reputations as colorful, homeless, and harmless characters even spread to the police, and this officer's cracking voice showed how genuinely affected the man felt.

The officer recounted pulling up in his car and discovering the bloodied remains of Hummingbird and Dragonfly on the sidewalk adjacent to their tent. A large knife lay near Hummingbird's outstretched fingers, leading the police to speculate that she tried to kill the animal, a wolf most likely, while attempting to save Dragonfly — a theory later verified by the one eyewitness to the killings — Babbling Betty, another homeless regular in the neighborhood who'd witnessed everything from her own tent on the sidewalk across the street.

Known by everyone from the patrol units to the local vendors, Terrence knew and liked Betty, a squat, big-eyed, round-bodied woman with a thick head sitting on shoulder-pad-sized shoulders and no visible neck in between. She wore her long, reddish-brown hair in a ponytail because, as she liked to say, "It makes me feel like a young girl."

The same reporter conducting the interview with the policeman now stood with her microphone in front of Betty, asking her to explain what she saw. Listening as she spoke in her usual rambling, nonstop way, Terrence felt a deep compassion for the woman as her squinting, murky blue eyes started watering. Terrence needed to wipe away his own tears as he listened to the description of the frightening scene.

"Terrible, terrible, can't explain it, never seen nothin' so scary, can't stop cryin', you know, they was my friends, good people, good people, didn't deserve what they got, no, no way, don't know what it was. I see a man walkin' toward 'em, and suddenly he's runnin' on all fours like a wolf or a coyote, maybe. We got coyotes around here, you know, and I was lookin' out my tent, such a nice night with stars and everything, and I see Dragonfly leavin' his tent and lookin' like he was gonna go pee, there's a spot behind that wall over there, and next thing I see is him gettin' jumped on and takin' down by that…that animal and he's screamin', screamin', somethin' terrible, you know. That's when I see Hummingbird comin' out of her tent with a knife, and she raises that knife and shouts real loud, but she didn't even make it more than a few steps before that animal jumped on her and killed her somethin' quick and vicious like. I didn't even hear her make a sound."

Betty closed her eyes, remaining silent as her bottom lip started quivering.

"Is there anything more you want to say, Betty?" the reporter asked.

"They was my friends, you know, good people, real good people, and I'm scared now, you know, real scared. Thought that wolf was gonna get me too when Tiger started barkin' and barkin', and when that wolf came closer, I peed myself. I don't mind tellin' you, I peed myself. But that thing kinda looked at Tiger, standin' there lookin' and lookin' and then ran away."

Betty held Tiger up to her face and kissed him on his head.

"Good ol' Tiger protectin' his mama, you know?"

Rapid blinking preceded the tears now streaming down her face.

"Tiger's a brave little dog, Betty," the reporter said, smiling at the white, black, and tan pug.

Cradling Tiger in the crook of her right arm, Betty nodded in agreement as she swiped the other forearm across her eyes and under her runny nose.

The interview ended. Terrence turned off the television and poured another drink.

CHAPTER TWENTY-FOUR
JUANA'S ANSWER

"Excuse me," Michael said, approaching Ramona's desk with the Sandy Koufax autobiography in his hand. "I'm looking for Terrence Covington. He's not answering his phone, so I'm wondering if he's here today."

Ramona dabbed the corners of her mouth with a napkin before placing her fork on the desk next to her half-eaten Chinese chicken salad.

"Terrence is here today," she answered. "He's probably on a lunch break, so you might find him where his wife is buried. He goes there a lot now. Do you know where her grave is?"

"Yes, I've been there before," Michael replied. "Thank you for your help."

Michael drove up the narrow pathway until he spotted Terrence's silver Toyota parked under the expansive, dark green canopy of a large oak tree. Easing his car behind it, he parked, grabbed the book from the passenger seat, and got out. Zigzagging in between other markers as he walked around the curved portion leading there, Michael stopped to gaze at Terrence kneeling over his wife's grave. Standing in silence about fifteen feet away, he decided to hold back and wait out of respect—but also to see what might happen next after he noted the recognizable pouch of marbles in Terrence's hand.

Michael wondered if Terrence would again place them in a Braille formation. Close enough to read them if he did and able to hear Terrence's voice, Michael's curiosity overrode his sense of guilt over this admitted invasion of privacy. On the verge of receiving the greatest shock of his life, Michael listened and observed.

***

Sitting on his knees, Terrence leaned over Juana's grave with his right arm raised, holding the pouch of marbles in the air. Juana's two-week inactivity notwithstanding, he continued to hope for a clue. If he could do something to stop the horrifying madness, something that started with the grisly murder of Francisco, he needed Juana to provide him with information that could lead somewhere. The rare and welcome silence of this midweek afternoon seemed almost therapeutic in its tranquility, even spiritual in its purpose, making Terrence feel that this time his plea might be answered.

"Are you still listening to me, Juana?" he asked, loud enough that Michael could hear.

Terrence waited, wondering if the sound of Juana's words would in some way drift toward him like a gentle breeze, renewing his spirit with hope. The surrounding quietness continued, from the silence of the birds to the idle neighboring streets.

"I'm losing faith," he told her. "I don't even know if

you're able to talk to me anymore."

Terrence closed his eyes, struggling to maintain hope in the face of his recent disappointment. Unable to prevent those nagging feelings of dread, he wondered if everything occurring marked the beginning of the horror rather than something ending soon.

"I don't know, maybe death offers a small window of opportunity to communicate before shutting it down," he said. "But it's gotten real bad out here, Juana. Real bad. I just lost two friends a couple of nights ago in such a terrible way. Two loving and kind, beat-up souls who somehow found and protected each other. If for no one else, I know I've got to keep trying to honor them. Hummingbird and Dragonfly."

Terrence lifted the pouch of marbles higher into the air like a torch, as if imitating the Statue of Liberty. With his grip tightening on the small bag, he whispered a prayer.

"God, I need you to help me. If there's something I can do, anything, let Juana give me the answer. Please."

Lowering his arm, Terrence opened the pouch and placed it on the grave.

"Here they are, Juana," he said. "I can't do anything else without you."

Terrence rose to his feet.

***

Observing all of this and hearing Terrence talk to his deceased wife as if speaking to her face-to-face, Michael felt a deep sense of sorrow for this good man's obvious love for her. As he started walking toward him, he suddenly came to an immediate halt after just a few steps. In confusion, he watched as Terrence started stumbling around again, just like the day they first met. This time, however, despite the lack of any shaking beneath his own feet, Michael didn't just witness Terrence drop to a knee, but he also noticed small yet discernable back-and-forth movements of the gravestone.

Michael looked behind him to glance at the surrounding trees. Every branch and leaf remained motionless. Spotting two squirrels in the tree to his right, he watched as they calmly continued munching on something as if they didn't have a care in the world. Yet right there in front of him, less than fifteen feet away, he couldn't deny the shaking ground around Terrence and Juana's grave. Without any understanding of this bizarre situation, he started approaching Terrence, wondering if the man needed help. Before uttering a word, however, a sudden strong jolt startled Michael, causing him to drop the book and lurch forward, tottering but not falling.

Moments later, the earthquake stopped.

Terrence's eyes widened in surprise at the sight of Michael. He didn't say anything as he scrambled back toward Juana's grave.

"Terrence," Michael said, speaking in an uncertain tone, "what just happened? It seems the ground was only shaking where you were and nowhere else. Maybe a city water line just burst. You think that might've caused it? Should you call your office?"

"Hold on, Michael," Terrence said, holding up a hand. "I need to see something."

Michael looked around him, his head still spinning. To his left, he saw two men in the distance dressed in biker gear standing by a grave. Each man held a bouquet of flowers. To his right, looking through the chain-link fence dividing the cemetery from the street, he saw a child and an adult behind a lemonade stand in front of a small house, talking to another adult. Neither the two men to his right nor the three people by the lemonade stand showed any type of visual concern that a strong earthquake occurred just moments before. This gave more credence to his speculation about a main line break. Underground city pipes were large and held a lot of water pressure, so maybe an explosion had occurred. Remaining hunched over Juana's grave, however, Terrence didn't seem to be in any hurry to find out.

Curious to see if he might spell something in Braille again, Michael took a few steps closer. Looking down, he gasped, staring in disbelief at the immediate discovery of Terrence watching the marbles move on their own—some rolling up, others down, and some straight ahead, one after the other.

"How are they moving like that, Terrence?" he asked, his unwavering eyes on the marbles. "That's a heck of a trick. A real good one."

Maintaining his laser-beam focus, Terrence hesitated before deciding to confess.

"The other messages from Juana," he said, "they only moved when the ground was shaking. This time it's different. They're still rolling."

Looking down on the marbles from a standing position, they reminded Michael of a marching band forming words in a halftime routine at a football game.

But these weren't people, they were marbles.

"Terrence, what are you talking about?" he asked. "You sound as if you think you're receiving messages from your wife."

The rolling stopped. Terrence now surveyed another Braille lineup, including the use of blues and yellows to go along with the ten black and ten white.

He stood and faced Michael.

"If I explained everything to you, believe me, you'll think I'm crazy," Terrence said. "Anyone would, and I wouldn't blame them. That's why I've kept this to myself. I was never going to say anything to anybody. But you're here now, Michael, and you've seen what just happened, so let me just do what I came here for. I've got Braille alphabet cards in my car, and I have to go get them. I need to figure out what Juana wrote."

Michael stared at him in confusion. Terrence seemed so sincere, so convincing, yet this couldn't possibly be real. Of course not. Yet...

"But how did you...when did you...? Michael cleared his throat. "I'm sorry," he said. "I just don't...understand how..."

Looking into Michael's eyes, Terrence paused before answering. "How any of this is possible?" he said, completing the question. "I'm still trying to figure it out myself. But I can't think about that right now. I don't have time. Juana's sending me another message, and it's her first one in weeks. From what I've been able to determine so far, I'm pretty sure she's warning me about something."

"Warning you?" Michael asked. "What kind of warning?"

"Something bad, that's all I can tell you," Terrence said. "And they started right before our gardening supervisor,

Francisco, was attacked and brutally killed by a wolf here in the cemetery. The man suffered a horrible death. Something unimaginable. And now the news is reporting more of that kind of killings."

Lowering his head, Michael started whispering something unintelligible that Terrence thought might be Hebrew. Maybe a prayer. When Michael looked up again, his eyes misting, Terrence observed his glazed expression of bewilderment and offered a gentle squeeze to his shoulder.

"I still don't know what I can do to help," Terrence said, "but Juana's been wanting me to know something, and those marbles are another message from her. I'm going to get those cards. I'll be right back."

Watching what just transpired left Michael feeling lightheaded, his legs unsteady. Someone communicating from the grave? Terrence was as sane as he was, so if seeing was believing, he now believed. But what did this mean?

From Michael's religious upbringing, learning about stories such as God conversing with Moses through a burning bush to write the Ten Commandments or ordering a willing Abraham to sacrifice his son, Isaac, he grew to embrace Judaism without accepting the authenticity of actual God-to-man conversations. In Michael's perspective, God was all about living your life by encouraging and spreading love rather than viewing Him, or Her, or It, as the Big Boss who kicks your butt if you don't behave.

As a Jewish religious leader, the question Michael struggled with the most centered on love's direct opposite: hate. The seemingly perpetual existence of man's inhumanity to man remained a timeless storm cloud engulfing every country in the world, and actions such as the recent spate of vile racist and religious killings underscored his questions about hate and human nature. How much control does God, the Creator, truly have over our everyday actions, and how much are we left to our own devices?

What Michael witnessed today was something he couldn't explain away as just another colorful story from the Old Testament. This occurred in Evergreen Cemetery, of all places, the eternal resting spot of Grandma Heddy and Grandpa Ben. Could they ever speak to him as Juana was doing with Terrence? Michael didn't know what to make of any of this, of the dizzying high wire he now balanced upon in his newly scrambled beliefs about life and death. Was there a second message meant to be conveyed here? One not just for Terrence from his wife, but from God to Michael?

Maybe those ancient stories from the Bible relied too much on believing the necessity of godly communication through conversation rather than something nonverbal. A Hebrew school teacher once scolded Michael for asking questions she thought ridiculous—if Moses grew up in a bilingual household, which language would God have chosen to speak, and why? The next question he asked her was if God wanted to speak to a deaf person, how would that be possible if they couldn't hear what was being said? Reflecting on his skepticism starting as that kid in Hebrew school, Michael now recognized that based on what he saw today, maybe a deaf person could somehow still communicate with God.

Today, through the simple gesture of lending a book to a friend, Michael sensed in his heart a divine guidance to come here at the time he did to see this actual miracle for himself.

Maybe Sandy Koufax, a fellow Jew, should be credited with aiding the spiritual growth of a rabbi. Whatever the reason, Michael now believed in the providence of helping Terrence through the apparent danger of this mystery—one dealing, unequivocally and equally, in life and death.

Being familiar with Braille, Michael realized what the marbles spelled, but one area still confused him. After Terrence returned and started searching through his alphabet cards, without understanding the reason for the letters spelling out what they did, Michael realized what the marbles meant—this was a name. Refraining from saying anything aloud, he remained quiet in consideration of Terrence's need to connect with his deceased wife.

Terrence turned his head away from the marbles and looked at Michael.

"You weren't supposed to be seeing any of this," he told him. "Or hearing any of what I said. Please respect that, Michael, and keep this between the two of us."

"You have my word."

With the addition of more yellows than before, Terrence's obvious anxiety grew with the larger amount of time required to search for previously unused letters. Michael decided that his friend's urgency to decipher Juana's message overrode his initial hesitancy to divulge the answer to whatever this whole thing was about.

***

Terrence heard a voice just above a whisper and, for a moment, wondered if, indeed, Juana's voice carried on the breeze. With initial disappointment, he realized the soft voice came from Michael.

Turning to look at him, he asked, "What did you say?"

"Naomi," Michael answered. "I'm almost one hundred percent certain that's what the marbles spell."

"Naomi?" Terrence repeated.

Kneeling at the gravesite again, Terrence said, "Naomi? Peter's mother? What about her, Juana? Can you tell me more?"

Terrence swept the marbles back into a pile next to the pouch. The ground didn't shake this time, but the marbles started rolling again. Neither man moved, staring in silence.

Terrence knew enough Braille now to recognize what the next word spelled.

"'Tell'?" he asked. "You want me to tell Naomi something? Is that it, Juana?"

Rubbing his hand through his hair, Terrence dropped down on an elbow and swept the marbles together with his other arm. Several more minutes of inactivity passed, and Terrence started collecting the marbles, frustrated at having to get back to work without an answer. Rising to his feet, a sudden revelation occurred to him, bringing him back to his knees and his face just inches from the grave.

"You want me to tell Naomi about Peter, is that it?" he asked. "You want me to understand she'll be able to hear me just like you can, right?"

With trembling hands, Terrence removed ten black and eight white marbles from the pouch and dropped them on the ground.

"Go on, Juana," he said. "If I'm right, I brought out the exact number of marbles you'll need to let me know. Are you telling me that Naomi will be able to hear what I say and she can save Peter's spirit from the Devil?"

The ground started shaking, but the vibration offered more of an easy, rocking motion now rather than a cause for sudden instability. Terrence remained on his knees with a slight smile appearing on his face as the moving marbles stopped in the formation he expected: five black and one white for the first letter, two black and four white for the second, and three black and three white for the final letter.

YES.

The confirmation of his hunch provided a brief sense of hope about stopping this horror, but a sudden question left him reeling, feeling like a drowning man without a life preserver.

If he spoke to Naomi's grave, telling her about Peter, how would Terrence know she heard him? And how would he find out if she wound up saving Peter after all?

When Terrence got to his feet, he turned to face Michael.

"I feel I owe you an explanation about how all of this started," he said. "Before Juana died, starting when her vision was OK to the time of almost total blindness, she used to play marble games with a kid who lives in our building, Nigel. It was kind of a babysitting thing, too, because his mother works. Nigel stayed with her after school. One day, after Juana died, I was about to leave for the cemetery to bring her flowers when Nigel approached me and asked if I'd bring the bag of marbles to her as a gift. Pretty nice thing for that young boy to do, huh?"

"Absolutely," Michael replied.

"After I placed the flowers on Juana's grave, I told her about Nigel's request. I put the marbles in a corner of the headstone. They were all inside the pouch at the time. Next thing I knew, the ground started shaking like we were having an earthquake. Then it stopped. I'd say less than a minute later, another one started happening. It wasn't a big jolt like the first one, but it lasted longer."

Terrence explained everything else to Michael, from the bouquet of flowers turning over repeatedly until reaching the side of the grave to the black and white marbles rolling out of the pouch until stopping in specific locations. He told him about taking a photo and discovering, almost by accident, that the marbles settled in spots that formed specific Braille letters.

"What did it say?" Michael asked.

"The three letters were 'D,' 'A,' and 'N,'" Terrence said. "At first, I thought Juana was referring to a man we know named Dan McIntyre. The next three-letter message I received, a 'G,' 'E,' and 'R,' completed the word. Dan was short for danger."

"Oh my God," Michael whispered.

"Each of the messages since then involved Naomi's son, Peter Levy, who died during World War II and is buried with his family near where Juana and I have our plots."

"I heard you mention his name today," Michael said. "Something about the Devil?"

"That's right," Terrence replied. "All of her completed messages until today's have told me that Peter Levy is evil and must be killed."

"Killed?" Michael asked, his eyes narrowing. "I'm stating the obvious here, but Peter Levy has been dead for a long time."

Terrence snorted a gust of air through his nose and then smiled.

"What can I say, Michael?" he said, shrugging his shoulders. "Welcome to my world, where my dead wife uses marbles to give me warnings in Braille about killing an evil young man who died in the War."

Nibbling on his upper lip, Michael took a deep breath. A worried expression followed.

"I don't yet know how I'm going to process what I saw and learned today," he said. "But I do know this will change how I think about a lot of things. As a rabbi and as a husband and father, it's something I'll keep to myself, just as you asked. This will always be between the two of us. But I won't be able to hide whatever changes may come over me in my daily life that I don't want to show—personal and professional. And that scares me, Terrence."

"I'm sorry you had to see this," he replied.

Michael shook his head. "Don't be," he told him. "I consider what I saw today to be the greatest blessing I could ever experience as a rabbi. Heck, that any person of faith could experience."

"If you say so," Terrence said.

"It raises as many questions as it answers," Michael told him, "but I think I'll be all right. At least, I hope I will."

"Well, I got nothin' but questions," Terrence said, "so whatever answers you come up with, make sure you share them with me."

Michael's brow wrinkled as his expression turned serious.

"With what you told me today, it's obvious there's

something urgent going on, and I want to help. If there's any assistance I can offer, let me know. The fact that I'm a rabbi and Peter Levy was Jewish may be a coincidence, but I'm starting to think I was meant to come here today, and it wasn't a coincidence at all. Just because God didn't have a conversation with me doesn't mean I'm not meant to do something."

Terrence extended his hand, and Michael did the same.

"Thank you, Michael," Terrence said. "I'm tired of dealing with the unknown and the warnings I've received by myself. I've decided I don't want to face this alone anymore. Can I ask a favor of you?"

"Of course," Michael said.

"The cemetery opens at seven o'clock each morning," he said, "but tomorrow, I'm going to come here at six to do what Juana told me to do—talk to Naomi Levy. Would you come with me? She was Jewish, too, I assume, so having a rabbi with me might be a benefit. If you can make it, I'll wait for you outside at the entrance gate."

"I wouldn't miss it for the world, Terrence," he answered. "I'll see you tomorrow morning, six o'clock."

"Thank you," Terrence said.

Michael held up his hand. "Hold on," he said. "I've got something for you."

Walking back a few feet beyond Juana's grave, Michael retrieved the book and extended his arm to give it to Terrence.

"Here's that book about Sandy Koufax I told you about," he said. "The Dodgers offered you a needed distraction during your Vietnam days, and maybe one of the best there ever was can offer you one now."

CHAPTER TWENTY-FIVE
A DEBATE WITH THE DEVIL

When Michael turned off his engine after following Terrence to the parking area the next morning, he observed him sitting in his car and staring through the windshield. After another minute, when Terrence got out and closed his door, Michael hurried over and placed his hand on his shoulder, wanting to offer reassurance.

"Juana is asking you to be the one to speak to Naomi Levy," he said, "but I'm here to support you. Even though your wife can't be here to stand next to you anymore, we both know her spirit certainly is. Let that be your source of strength."

Terrence nodded.

Michael took a couple of steps back and faced him. "The way I see it, what you're about to do shows Juana's continual connection with you and your faith in that connection. You believe in her. That's all that matters, and that's why you're here. I know you have your doubts about whether anything good will come from this, but let her be your guide. Feel her here with you. There's a purpose to all of this. There must be."

***

With Michael standing in silence by his side, Terrence faced Naomi Levy's headstone. The above-average warmth of the early morning air already signaled the forthcoming heat and humidity of this September day, exacerbating Terrence's nervousness. He lacked the confidence to believe he could somehow succeed in reaching the spirit of a woman who died in 1952, but Juana's appeal needed to be obeyed. Of that, he felt certain.

Removing a piece of paper from his pocket, Terrence started reading the first couple of lines of a full-page letter he'd written to Naomi the night before. After glancing at all the remaining sentences, however, he crumpled the note and stuffed it back in his pants pocket. He wanted to speak from the heart and in the moment.

Staring at the thin, round-eyed, round-faced woman looking out from the photograph on her marker, his eyes settled on hers as if they were facing each other in person. Terrence drew a deep breath, bracing himself to speak to an invisible spirit if such a thing truly existed.

"Naomi?" he said, his soft voice tentative. "Naomi Levy? My name is Terrence Covington. I work here at the cemetery. My wife, Juana, recently passed away and is buried near you and your family. And I will join her there one day."

Terrence paused, not with any expectation of a reply but rather to gather his thoughts about Peter, which he now needed to convey.

"Your son, Peter, needs your help. I don't know if there's really a Devil or not, but something inhuman and powerful has taken over his spirit, or soul, or whatever the afterlife is, causing people to die in a horrible way, using your son as a source of evil to carry out the murders."

Terrence stood in silence, nibbling on his lip at his uncertainty of what to say next. His eyes moved from Naomi's photograph to that of Peter's, showing a man possessing eyes and a face shaped like his mother's, with those eyes enhanced by the strategically tilted placement of the bill from his airman's cap, ending just above the eyebrows.

The contrast of a plain-looking, frail mother next to her handsome son's commanding physical presence struck him as something bittersweet. Here was a strapping military man who came into this world through this woman's nurturing womb and whose first experience of life and love was her. Terrence suddenly realized what he needed to say.

"You're Peter's mother," he said. "You brought him into this world. You were his mother in life but also in death. Maybe as a grown man, as a war hero, he didn't need you to protect him, but he needs you now more than ever. Find him and bring him back to you, Naomi. You must save Peter's soul."

In the ensuing silence, Terrence glanced at Michael, standing with hands clasped and head bowed. The whispered phrases he spoke sounded like the same language Terrence had heard from him before. This time, Terrence felt certain it was a Hebrew prayer.

Adjacent to a tall palm tree about twenty feet away, a sudden, loud rustling from the shrubbery to their right shattered the solitude, startling both men. Swinging their heads around to look, they didn't see anything unusual. With his thoughts shifting into overdrive about the wolf attack on Francisco, Terrence's body stiffened, frightened by the impossibility of preventing a similar savage occurrence from happening to them. Sensing Michael's nervousness, Terrence experienced a deep feeling of regret for inviting him.

But it was too late now.

After another minute of silence, Terrence started breathing easier, relieved that it must have been an overreaction to a harmless animal or bird. Returning his attention to Naomi's grave, he focused on her photograph again.

"I don't know what to do next, Naomi," he said. "Are you listening to me? Are you hearing what I'm saying?"

A deep, raspy voice torpedoed the silence.

"I hear you."

Both men spun around again, finding themselves staring at a shadowy figure behind the same shrubbery. With only his upper half exposed and his lower half blocked by the height of the shrubs, they gazed at a Caucasian man with short brown hair wearing a zippered jacket covering most of his white-collared shirt.

"Excuse me, but the cemetery isn't open to the public until seven o'clock," Terrence said, sensing something peculiar, even dangerous, about the man. "How did you get in?"

"My mother is nothing but a lost, wandering spirit, Terrence," the man said, his voice tinged with menace. "How will she be able to find me if she can't recognize me?"

"I don't know what you're talking about, mister," Terrence replied, a sudden dryness enveloping his throat.

"And how did you know my name? Do you know someone who works with me?"

"Who are you?" Michael asked. "What do you want?"

A creeping smile appeared on the man's face before transforming into a condescending sneer.

"Well, well, if it isn't the good Rabbi Michael Feinman," the man said. "Religious leader to a doomed race."

"Excuse me?" Michael said. "What did you just say?"

Crossing his arms, the man continued. "You know, Rabbi, when it comes to the great religions, anti-Semitism has always been my favorite denomination. I find it so...*appealing*. To be part of such an important, historical movement dedicated to your people's demise, gives me hope for the future of mankind."

Holding out his hands like a preacher on a pulpit, the man added, "It's taken longer than I expected, Rabbi, and we haven't gotten there yet, but you and your people will finally wind up on the wrong side of history one day." The man elicited a mocking chuckle. "But the right side of history to me."

Michael took a step forward, glaring at this stranger making racist, arrogant comments.

"A history that has proven time and again that no matter what we've gone through, the Jewish people have survived and will continue to survive," Michael replied, working to suppress his rage. "In case you and your neo-Nazi pals haven't read your history books, your king, your führer, is long dead. And how did that happen? Hiding away in a bunker like someone who lost his nerve, a man who kills himself rather than acting as a true commander with guts and leading his soldiers until the end. No, not him. Instead, he leaves his loyal followers to suffer the results of his decisions. Even young boys and old men. To use an appropriate war term, the guy went missing in action, abandoning his post at a time when he was needed the most. And yet, I don't know why, he's still your hero. Still the poster boy for you and all your other racist fanatics."

The man raised his face to the skies and roared with laughter, clapping hard with wide, exaggerated, back-and-forth motions of his hands.

"Bravo, Rabbi Feinman, bravo," he shouted. "A lovely speech. So eloquent and heartfelt. But despite doing my part for their just cause and being a longtime supporter, I'm not a neo-Nazi. You may think I am, but you have no idea who you're dealing with. No idea what you're dealing with." Smiling, he added, "Soon, but not yet."

As the man approached, seemingly gliding through the bushes with the ease of walking through a swinging door, Terrence's heart started racing when he recognized Peter's face. Staring at the reality of Juana's warning, his thoughts enveloped him in a whirlpool of dread.

"Do you know who I am, Terrence?" Peter asked.

Terrence stared, tongue-tied, as he studied the face of a dead man somehow standing before him and asking questions.

"I've been following your conversations with Juana," he said. "Very clever how she spoke to you, I must give credit where it's due. That woman possessed a strong sense of things to come, and even in death, that power survived. So here I am, Terrence. The one she warned you about. Peter Levy, Act

Two."

Upon closer inspection, Terrence realized that the face and eyes of the young, good-looking military man in the photograph didn't quite match the face of the man in front of him. The expressive blue eyes full of life in the gravestone photo now appeared bloodshot with a sickly liquid casing. The skin's pallid tone bordered on colorless, and his mouth appeared a bit crooked, like someone who'd suffered a stroke.

Peter smiled, exposing uneven and rotting, yellowish-brown teeth.

"Not quite the same handsome man I was, but I got what I wanted. A new soul and a new life."

"Are you…the Devil?" Terrence asked.

Laughing in response, Peter ended with a sound more like the yipping of a hungry animal celebrating a kill.

"I've had this conversation too many times in my ancient life," he said, "and I don't feel like answering it again. Let's just say that the God you believe in lost the ability to oversee everything all the time a long time ago, and that's where we came in. Every day of every year for every succeeding generation, society's grip on civility weakened and eroded like a crumbling mountain, and you can thank us for that. It's a war of good versus evil, and your God is fighting a losing battle. The day can't come soon enough when the outcome is finally determined."

***

Michael stiffened, hearing the thoughts he pondered previously concerning the possible limits of God's abilities for humanity put into words.

"And what outcome is that?" he asked.

Peter chuckled, his patronizing expression antagonizing Michael further.

"That's an easy one to answer, Rabbi," he said. "When virtue is seen as a vice, we win. When kindness and respect are interpreted as signs of weakness, we win. When distrust and animosity define man's thoughts toward his fellow man, we win."

Peter spread out his hands, palms up.

"It's obvious we're already winning," he said. "Think about it. Does anyone other than the truly naïve take the expression, 'Peace on Earth, goodwill toward men,' as anything other than a laughable phrase uttered at Christmas? Cynicism is now baked into the cake, and the world I see isn't just nibbling on it. They're gorging."

With the back of his hand, Michael wiped away newly formed beads of sweat from his forehead, scowling as his eyes lasered in on Peter's.

"I've always believed there are a lot more good people in this world than those like you," Michael told him. "But good people who just want to live in peace and raise their families don't make headlines. They don't get people talking. Evil deeds are isolated things, but they're so often big, and bold, and terrible that they dominate the news and make it seem like societies are breaking down everywhere. But when the blaring lights shining on those stories finally fade away, as they always do, what happens after that? The normalcy that presided over most things anyway takes center stage again and resumes its rightful place in people's everyday lives. Family, friendships, schools, and the workplace. And those evil facts of life that occasionally hit us like a thunderstorm are seen again as what they always were: the exception to the norm, not the other way around."

Smirking, Peter asked, "Are you finished, Rabbi Feinman? You're boring me with your insipid talk."

"If I am," Michael said, "it's only because you refuse to consider anything but what you already believe. The fact that mankind has continually survived through thousands of years of despots and cruelty and poverty and disease convinces me that you're never going to come out on top. You're a false prophet who's only fooling yourself. Of that, I've never been more certain."

Peter stared in silence at Michael, his eyes narrowing into an intense glare.

"There are many like me, Rabbi, more than you can imagine. We're part of a growing legion of millions throughout the world, a spreading bacterium that will eventually topple that heavenly tree that you and every other religion refer to as God, no matter what name is given. And when we do, when that tree finally comes crashing down, the good that remains in mankind will wither and die like the leaves on that fallen tree, replaced by perpetual anarchy of the soul."

Rubbing his hands together, Peter smiled. "And that will be a truly blessed event."

***

A heavy silence hung in the air.

"Why did you choose Peter Levy?" Terrence asked. "Is this going to happen to others, too? Will it happen to me when I die? Will it happen to Juana?"

"We have our reasons for who we choose," Peter answered. "Right now, I don't see any reason why you or your wife won't be resting in eternal peace."

Terrence turned away, needing to gather his thoughts and recover his fortitude. At that moment, however, he heard Peter's voice take on a sudden sinister tone with the ominous words he spoke next.

"How does eternal peace sound right now, Terrence? Juana is waiting."

"Leave him alone!" Michael shouted.

Terrence reached out and squeezed Michael's arm. "Thanks," he said, "but I never backed down from a fight in my life, and I ain't startin' now."

Terrence stared into Peter's cold, lifeless eyes. "Let him go. You came for me, not him."

"I'm here for a reason, Terrence," Michael said, his eyes fixed on Peter. "I'm convinced of it. I'm not going anywhere."

"Enough!" Peter shouted.

Unzipping his jacket and throwing it to the ground, Peter exposed a torn white shirt shorn of any buttons. His eyes darting back and forth between the two men, he quickly kicked off his shoes, revealing his bare feet. Leering at them with an expression of unnerving ferocity, his hairy-chested, muscular frame now uncovered, Peter's voice transformed from a deep-throated timbre into a demonic growl.

"Die!"

The bravado of both men shriveled away as they stood motionless, suddenly imprisoned by the terror of Peter's facial metamorphosis into monstrous, distorted, wolflike features of blood-red eyes and an elongated mouth baring curved, spiked teeth. Dropping to the ground, Peter's physical change took full form, and all semblance of a human disappeared under the hairy torso. Michael shut his eyes, hurriedly whispering a Hebrew prayer of protection from Psalm 91. Terrence braced himself for the full expectation of immediate and painful death as the final moments of his life.

Until something happened, unforeseen and proving unbreakable.

CHAPTER TWENTY-SIX
LULLABY

Neither Terrence nor Michael heard Naomi's pleas, but Peter did.

"Peter! My son! No!"

Terrence dropped to the ground, unaware of Peter's sudden change in behavior. Throwing his hands and arms over his head, he knocked into the side of Michael's prostrate body as he prayed, waiting for the end to come and hoping his suffering could be as brief as possible.

Remaining unnoticed by the two men, Peter's transformation back to an upright position stopped halfway between the human he appeared to be previously and the wolflike, four-legged figure he was moments before.

"Who are you to tell me what to do?" the thing inside Peter bellowed, his growling voice monstrous yet comprehensible. "You took your son from me once, but he's mine now. He does as I command, and you're powerless to stop us."

"Peter, I know you can hear me," Naomi said. "I have

finally found you, and I've come to take you home."

"I control him now, Naomi. I am Peter, and he is me! Peter… is… me!"

"Peter, my dear, sweet son, listen to me. You are there, inside, and I know you can hear me. I am your mother, and I will always love you. That evil spirit is not you. It's not you. You are kind and decent. You are full of love. You are not the wicked and immoral creature this thing wants you to be. Come back to me, Peter, come back, and we'll join your father and sister in eternal peace."

***

As several moments passed, Terrence's awareness of something unusual occurring started coming into focus. Glancing at Michael, alive, untouched, and curled up on his side with his hands partially covering his face, Terrence lifted a portion of his arm to peek out. Realizing that this thing in Peter's body seemed to be conversing with someone not there, resembling a mentally ill street person, he nudged Michael to look for himself.

"What's going on?" Michael whispered.

"I don't know," Terrence said, keeping his voice low. "Maybe we can escape if he stays distracted."

Alternately on their elbows and knees, they began to slide back little by little, the two men keeping their attention on Peter, hoping to remain unnoticed for another minute before making a break for it to their cars.

"Peter lives through me now," the angry thing inside him growled. "He's mine, and his spirit will do as I command. Watch and observe his fate, Naomi. Death is coming, and I will prove how powerless you are."

Peter turned toward the two men, who both were aware that an insufficient amount of time remained to make a running escape possible. Growling and licking his lips, Peter's eyes glowed an angry red. Covering their heads again, the numbing fear surged in Terrence and Michael.

***

Naomi's spirit seemed to falter. The beginnings of doubt emerged, weakening her resolve to conquer this malevolent force that had made a helpless captive of her son. Was she destined to lose Peter for eternity as she lost him in life?

"Naomi, my child," a familiar voice said, "I am here with you now as I told you I would be."

In immediate recognition, Naomi listened to the words of Bunica Sofia.

"What can I do?" Naomi asked. "Look what's happened to my beautiful, loving son. Will Peter's spirit be lost to me forever? Will he never be a part of his family again?"

"I made a vow to you in Bucharest that we would defeat this evil," Bunica Sofia said. "Do you remember?

"Yes, yes, I do remember," she replied. "But that thing is controlling Peter, and he will kill those poor men now if we don't do something."

"Sing with me, child."

As Bunica Sofia started singing the same Romanian lullaby she once had to lull a crying baby Petre to sleep almost one hundred years before, Naomi joined her, the two voices rising in volume and blending in sweet, soulful harmony.

"Hai Luluțu dormi un picu..."

***

With his arms still covering his head as he lay flat on the

ground, Michael started hearing the faint sound of two women's voices singing, of all things, his favorite childhood lullaby, "Cantec de Leagan." Remaining stationary and hearing the volume of the voices increase, he wondered if this was somehow meant to be a goodbye fragment of his life, offering a last beautiful memory before death.

As each second passed, and the continuation of the voices moved on from one line to the next, Michael gathered the courage to lift his head and survey the situation. He saw Terrence doing the same thing, supporting himself on his elbows and looking toward the irate monster, still yelling as if someone stood there arguing with him.

With the voices of the duet now clearly audible in his head, Michael realized through Terrence's unchanging facial expression that the man wasn't hearing any singing as he was. For Michael, however, hearing a lullaby so deeply personal from somewhere beyond his understanding represented something empowering and significant. A sudden feeling of bravado and defiance overtook him. As Terrence watched in fear and shock, Michael rose to his feet and stood erect. Lifting his head in dreamy reminiscence, he started singing in full-throated unison with the two voices.

"Dormi in pace..."

Naomi and Bunica Sofia continued singing the lullaby, the urgency highlighted by the passion of their voices. The wolflike thing snarled and drooled as it moved toward Michael, exposing teeth intent on devouring flesh.

"Michael, what are you doing?" Terrence yelled. "Stop it!"

**

After another few seconds, brushing a hand across his eyes in confusion, Terrence stared in astonishment as the wolflike thing, seemingly on the verge of attacking Michael, suddenly broke into a crazed, furious sprint around the Levy graves. Yelping and snapping, its speed continuing to increase, it suddenly leaped into the air and landed on its belly, flailing and beating its furry fists while grunting unintelligible sounds.

He didn't know what to make of it, but Terrence seemed to recognize an unexplainable link between Michael's singing and the monster's complete change in behavior. As he would soon observe, it signaled the harbinger of a sudden, strange, and unexpected phenomenon.

Losing the wolflike features, the skin on the thing's face started flaking away, leaving layers of hairy, fleshy remains on the ground. What was once Peter's face turned into a white, wrinkled mass of oozing flesh, the blazing red and yellow eyes still glowering at Terrence and Michael. Michael's singing stopped as the monster shuffled backward toward the Levy graves, stopping at the foot of Naomi's.

In a raspy, defiant voice, the thing bellowed, "Ah, yes, 'Cantec de Leagan.' A baby's lullaby in Bucharest. A dead man's lullaby in Los Angeles." The monster leaned down closer. "You may have found a way to recapture your son, Naomi, but hear me now. There will be many more Peters to possess and control, so we'll keep coming. I'm just one of millions. From birth to death, to the afterlife, we're in a war, and however long it takes, we will be victorious."

Terrence heard this thing's words loud and clear and sensed something good, something hopeful. But the murderous figure, with skin looking like a melted candle, still stood in front of them, able to strike and kill at any second. Closing his eyes, Terrence whispered a prayer.

"God, if this is the end, thank you for all the good things in my life. Please let me rest in peace with Juana."

"Terrence," the soft voice whispered, "my love, you're going to be fine. I promise you."

Terrence jerked his head to the left and then the right, hoping to see someone who wasn't there.

"Juana?" he whispered.

Moving toward the foot of Peter's grave, the monster, once resembling Naomi's son, turned and stood in silence with its back to the monument and its arms at its sides. Several seconds later it fell backward, landing on the ground in rigid stiffness, with its head situating under the center of Peter's World War II photograph. Starting with small, jerky motions, the body started moving as if having a mild seizure before escalating into wild gyrations from the head to the chest, arms, legs, and feet.

When the frenzied gestures stopped, Terrence stared in awe after realizing the body now lay halfway in the ground. Moments later, in a sudden flash of yellow, red, and orange, the previous inhabitant of Peter Levy's body and the possessor of his spirit burst into an ovular-shaped ball of flames lasting a mere few seconds before disappearing and drifting away on the wings of a vapory blur. In its wake, an outline of the body remained etched in the soil, and fiery remnants of the pants burned like scattered memorial candles honoring the fallen. Terrence and Michael remained motionless, staring out into the nothingness.

Gathering his wits and then his thoughts as to the

outcome of all this, Terrence reflected on the words he heard the monster say. Maybe, somehow, Naomi's spirit ended up saving Peter after all. And in saving Peter's soul in the afterlife, Terrence fully understood the significance for Michael and him. Naomi saved their lives as well.

Terrence wiped away a tear, suddenly feeling the enormity of everything that had transpired, from Juana's first warning through today's life-threatening moments of terrible fear and expected death. Terrence thought about Hummingbird and Dragonfly, reflecting again on their nightmarish end.

"If there's a next life," he whispered, "I hope you guys catch a break."

"I won't ever get over this, Terrence," Michael said, narrowing his eyes as he gazed into the distance. "But it's given me renewed faith in God as a force to be reckoned with. Maybe we're taken on as teammates in the afterlife to help fight battles like these."

Terrence placed his hand on Michael's shoulder.

"From now on, when I'm sitting in church, I think I'll sing those hymns with a little more purpose, imagining Juana is there with me. Who knows, maybe she really will be."

Michael smiled. "Before I leave," he said, "I'm going to go visit my Grandma Heddy and Grandpa Ben. After all that's happened, I've got something I want to say to them. And to ask them."

Glancing at the time on his watch, Terrence couldn't believe that with everything that had transpired, only fifty minutes had passed since he first arrived at Evergreen. The cemetery wouldn't open for another ten minutes.

"We open at seven," Terrence said, "so if you don't mind waiting by the gate, someone from the office will let you out. If they ask how you got in, just tell them who you are and that I met you here early so you could recite a prayer at your grandparents' graves. As for me, I'd like a little privacy if you don't mind. How can I not go talk to Juana?"

"Of course," Michael said. "And on behalf of so many people who will never know their lives were saved, please thank her for me. And may she forever rest in peace."

As Michael headed toward his car, Terrence called out to him.

"What was that singing all about?" he asked. "I damn near wanted to kill you myself when you stood up like that, singing your fool head off."

Michael laughed. "Yeah, I guess I must have surprised you pretty good with that, didn't I?" he said. He turned his head downward in thought before answering further.

"It's a Romanian lullaby my grandma sang to me when I was a kid," he answered. "For some reason, I felt it was the right thing to do at that moment. When death is staring you in the face, and the end can happen in the next instant, it's impossible to know what you might do until you do it. You experienced that in Vietnam, and now I know it, too. I've learned that when you hear the angels sing, it must be for a good reason, so don't be afraid to sing along with them."

CHAPTER TWENTY-SEVEN
FARTHER, EVER FARTHER, FROM THE STREET

Hands in his pockets, Michael stood over the graves of Heddy and Benjamin in meditative silence before speaking to them.

"Remember when I used to laugh at those silly clichés you said, like, 'Don't cry over spilled milk,' or 'He who laughs last laughs best?' Or one that I admit to saying to my own kids sometimes: 'When life gives you lemons, make lemonade'? And then what you would tell me when I rolled my eyes after hearing you say them? That those old expressions are around because situations in life keep happening to make them still true?"

Michael's eyes started watering. Pausing to wipe them and regain his composure, he continued. "I don't recall you ever saying the one about how life is a mystery, but I'll tell you one I've always considered to be the ultimate mystery: What happens to us when we die? You discovered the answer years ago, of course, but I never dwelled on it much before, even as a rabbi who presided over numerous funeral services and comforted the many who grieved."

Michael stared at Heddy's marker and then at Benjamin's, rereading their birth and death dates and reflecting on that beautiful poem by Linda Ellis titled "The Dash," signifying that person's life lived between those two dates.

"Yeah, I know life is a mystery, too. From one day to the next, none of us know for sure what's going to happen. God laughs as man plans, right? Well, one thing we do know for certain is that life ends eventually for everyone, and although I've never heard any kind of cliché about death being a mystery, I at least know something about life. And in my mind, Grandma and Grandpa, after seeing what I've seen here at Evergreen Cemetery, in this same place where you reside, death is much more of a mystery now than I ever realized."

Rolling his tongue in a slow slide across the inside of his upper lip, Michael reflected on all that had happened. The sound of car engines outside the cemetery gates and the chirping birds inside announced the beginning of another day in the city.

"I've always told the members of my temple who lost a loved one that they should believe that the person who died can still hear you. I really didn't believe that, but if it offers comfort to someone who's grieving, why not, right?"

Michael chuckled and shook his head.

"Well, I'm a believer now, not just because of what I witnessed, but also because of what I heard. I don't know where those singing voices were coming from, or who they were, but 'Cantec de Leagan'? Really? The lullaby you sang to me as a child somehow helping to save my life today?"

Michael took a deep breath, holding it in for several moments before exhaling with a final sense of relief at the life-changing and life-saving events of the morning.

"Standing here talking with you now, Grandpa and Grandma, and thinking of death as something more mysterious than I ever imagined, I'll leave here today with another unsolved mystery—one I'm now considering as entirely possible.

"Can you hear me?"

***

Before returning to Juana's gravesite, Terrence stopped in front of Naomi's grave, wanting to thank her for saving his life if, indeed, the events he witnessed and the words he heard meant the end of this horrific ordeal. With tentative steps, he approached her grave and looked again into the eyes of the woman on the headstone's photograph. From his earlier feelings of a slender, ordinary-looking woman, he now saw a remarkable person of great substance, toughness, and incredible defiance. Most of all, he saw a mother who possessed an eternity's worth of love for her son.

"Thank you, Naomi," he said. "Where I faced death today and accepted my fate in fear, you faced something far worse and wouldn't accept any other outcome than saving your son's soul. I think you did that, and me talking to you now, so grateful to be alive, is proof of your victory."

Closing his eyes, Terrence hung his head and offered a prayer for the entire Levy family to rest as one in eternal peace. Lifting his gaze to move to Peter's grave, intending to look at the face of the real man, he stopped, and stared, and lost all sense of time or space to what he saw.

In slow, crumbling increments, Terrence observed the recently blank, gray marble section of Peter's death date start breaking away as if by some invisible chisel. No sound emanated from the marker, just a silent, bit by bit chipping away until the reappearance of the date, August 1, 1943, dispelling any doubt about whether Naomi had been reunited with her son. Terrence walked over and kneeled by the headstone, collecting some of the fallen pieces and placing them in his pocket. Putting them in a bag next to the pouch of marbles in his drawer suddenly seemed like the right thing to do. Staring at the result of this spiritual event, his breathing grew more rapid until the dam of his emotions broke, freeing his pent-up tears to flow.

Like a crying baby in need of a lullaby.

***

"It's over, Juana," Terrence said, kneeling at her grave. "Maybe one day I'll understand how it all worked, how you could move the marbles and talk to me. But all I know is that without you, so much more would have happened, so many terrible things."

He smiled, leaning forward to kiss the ground before rising to his feet.

"I'll keep bringing the marbles and leaving them here so we can talk," he said. "Even a couple of words here and there, OK?"

The ground started shaking before Terrence took his first step toward the car. Turning back to the grave, he watched the marbles roll from the pouch until they formed a four-letter word. Terrence no longer required the alphabet cards, and what he read broke his heart.

OVER.

Wiping a tear, Terrence stood over Juana's grave and nodded.

"I think I understand, Juana," he said. "Something tells me that you communicated with me to save my life. And in doing that, you did so much more. Maybe Peter will thank you one day. After all, you're neighbors now."

Terrence looked around in appreciation of another sunny day as he watched and listened to birds swooping from tree to tree, singing from the branches. He felt a strong sense of a life still open to memorable experiences, and he looked forward to every one of them.

"I guess it's time to start bringing you flowers again, Juana," he said, smiling. "I love you and always will. Forever."

Terrence stooped to collect the marbles, but before reaching them, they started moving again. Straightening up in surprise, he watched as Juana spelled out her final word. With each letter of the four that formed, the bittersweet tears welling up in Terrence's eyes didn't stop his smile from growing wider until a hearty laugh sounded as he stared at Juana's reply:

MORE.

***

After Terrence parked his car near the office and got out, he spotted something unusual, causing him to pause and look closer. On the passenger side, several feet above the hood, a hummingbird with a white, speckled throat, a white-tipped tail, and a shining green body flew and floated overhead near a hovering and zigzagging blue iridescent dragonfly. Terrence admired the beauty of their aerial ballet until they zoomed farther, ever farther from the street, toward the lush green trees in the distance.

He watched. He wondered. He wished.

He walked away.

THE END

Author's Note

Despite the courageous heroism displayed by the airmen during Operation Tidal Wave in WWII, including the awarding of five Medals of Honor, the mission turned out to be at least as much about tragedy as triumph. With the initial protests from group commanders disregarded, of the 177 Liberator bombers departing from the airfields of Benghazi on that fateful August morning, only 92 returned. Over 300 US airmen were killed, and the Germans captured more than 100 others. Approximately 80 more men were captured and held prisoner in Turkey after their planes were forced to land there. Although much damage was inflicted on the oil refineries during the raid, the Germans repaired many of them, and they were operating again within several weeks.

Other Books Available by
Keith Steinbaum

A tragic, life-changing event occurred in my mid-teens that transformed me into a creative writer. After a decade-long attempt at becoming a professional song lyricist, and despite having several songs recorded in various parts of the world, I eventually embarked on a long career in the landscape industry.

It was during this period that I started writing my first novel, The Poe Consequence, a story originally inspired by the number of gang affiliated housing areas I worked at. The book went on to be included in Kirkus Reviews' 'The Best Books of 2015' year-end issue, winner of the 2021 Book Excellence Awards for Best Fiction Novel, winner of the 2022

Maincrest Media Book Awards, winner of the 2024 Global Book Awards for the Suspense Action Fiction category, and winner of the 2024 American Fiction Book Awards for the Horror: Paranormal/Supernatural category.

My second book, You Say Goodbye, originally inspired by a story in the obituary section about Alexandra Scott from the Alex's Lemonade Stand Foundation, was selected as the 2020 winner of the TopShelf Book Awards for Best Fiction/Intrigue, winner of the 2022 Maincrest Media Book Awards for the Mystery/Suspense category, winner of the 2024 Global Book Awards for the Traditional Detective Mysteries category, and a finalist in the Book Excellence Awards competition.

My third novel, In Lieu of Flowers, is my first with World Castle Publishing LLC and was inspired by a remarkable event that happened to my grandfather as an infant in the late 1800s in Bucharest, Romania. The book placed as a finalist in the 2024 American Fiction Book Awards for the Horror: Paranormal/Supernatural category, and also received a finalist placing in the Chanticleer International Book Awards for the Paranormal Fiction category.

www.ingramcontent.com/pod-product-compliance
Lightning Source LLC
Chambersburg PA
CBHW031912190626
46814CB00003BA/863